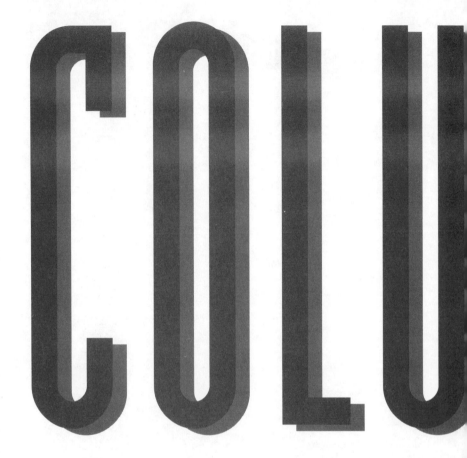

COLU

William

A TOM DOHERTY ASSOCIATES BOOK
NEW YORK

Based on the Universal Television Series COLUMBO
Created by Richard Levinson & William Link

MBO

THE GLITTER MURDER

Harrington

FORGE

COLUMBO: THE GLITTER MURDER
A novel by William Harrington
Based on the Universal Television series COLUMBO
Created by Richard Levinson & William Link

This book is printed on acid-free paper.

A Forge Book
Published by Tom Doherty Associates, Inc.
175 Fifth Avenue
New York, NY 10010

Forge® is a registered trademark of Tom Doherty
Associates, Inc.

Library of Congress Cataloging-in-Publication Data

Harrington, William.
    Columbo : the glitter murder / William Harrington.
        p.   cm.
    "A Tom Doherty Associates book."
    ISBN 0-312-86161-3
    I. Title.
  PS3558.A63C647   1997
  813'.54—dc21   96-24271
                                                      CIP

First Edition: March 1997

Printed in the United States of America

0 9 8 7 6 5 4 3 2 1

ONE

THURSDAY, JULY 2

Everyone who saw it was intrigued by the name on the masthead of *Glitz:* Ai-ling Cooper-Svan, Publisher and Editor-in-Chief.

The name Ai-ling was of course Chinese. The famous Soong sisters had been Ch'ing-ling, who married Sun Yat-sen, Mei-ling, who married Chiang Kai-shek, and Ai-ling, who married H. H. Kung. This Ai-ling was named for her great-grandmother, the daughter of an enormously wealthy Cantonese merchant. Ai-ling's grandmother, too, had been Chinese, the daughter of a Shanghai merchant. The dowries brought by these two Chinese brides had contributed hugely to the Cooper family fortune. The business alliances the marriages had cemented had contributed even more.

Cooper was the name of a family of tough Yankee ship owners and traders who, generation after generation, had sent sailing ships, then steamships, to Canton and Shanghai.

Svan was the name of the Swedish film director she had married. She had kept her maiden name and hyphenated it with Svan's because she had no intention of dropping the name Cooper for the name Svan.

Most people called her Eileen, as they had begun to do when she was in college, because they were uncertain just how to pronounce Ai-ling—which was not so difficult; it was Eye-ling.

Ai-ling Cooper-Svan sat behind her desk in the office of the publisher and editor-in-chief of *Glitz*. She was more often described as handsome than as beautiful. She had straight black hair styled to curve under her ears, dark eyes, and a compact body that was trim and taut. Her slender hips and legs and her flat bottom were the envy of women known as greater beauties. Her face was round, with a pug nose. Her erect posture and direct, blunt manner suggested hauteur. They were perhaps an element of her inheritance from people who had been immodestly proud: the Coopers for five or six generations, the Chinese ancestors for fifty.

If she had a defect—and she did have a conspicuous one—it was that she smoked three or more packs of cigarettes a day. She was constantly lighting, puffing, flicking ash, and disposing of butts. She sprayed her breath often, but her hair, skin, and clothes stank of tobacco smoke. What was more, she hacked. But she couldn't stop smoking; she was addicted. She was thirty-six and had been smoking for twenty years. For her, the warnings were too late.

As publisher of a magazine that emphasized style, she was herself an image of style. This morning she wore a suit of Lincoln green: a soft hip-length jacket that had no buttons and could not be closed, with tapered pants; also a white shirt with open collar and French cuffs.

She owned the magazine. She had bought it eight years ago, out of her inheritance, and had turned it from a Los Angeles tabloid into a slick monthly magazine, every issue filled with scented cards advertising perfumes, colognes, and aftershave lotions. Unlike her father, who lived idly, rapidly dissipating his inheritance, Ai-ling was dissipating hers only slowly. In the eight years she had owned it, *Glitz* had earned a profit only once. It had broken even, roughly, three years; and it had lost money four years. It had not lost much, though. What was more important to her, *Glitz* had made her someone to be reckoned with. She had never set out to ruin anyone and had never done it; but to be ignored by *Glitz* was a decided disadvantage in the film industry, in the world of art and music, and even in California politics.

Her desk was a kidney-shaped glass table: a heavy glass top sitting on glass pedestals. Spread over it was a batch of photographs: twenty-five or thirty eight-by-ten color prints. She had divided them into three piles: accepted, possible, rejected.

She picked up the telephone on the credenza and told her secretary to call Bill Lloyd and tell him she wanted to see him.

While she waited for Lloyd, she lit another Marlboro and moved pictures from pile to pile.

Her telephone, her ashtray, her carafe were on the credenza, together with half a dozen autographed pictures. She kept nothing on the glass desk but pictures and papers she was currently working on. People who worked for her knew better than to drop files on her desk. They handed them to her, and she put them where she wanted them.

"Ah . . . William," she said when Lloyd came in. "Look at these. What should we use?"

Lloyd knew her well enough to guess at a glance which pile of photos was which. He leaned forward but did not put his hands on her desk and make smudges on the glass. He frowned and pursed his lips.

They were pictures of Beverly Tree. She was playing the female lead in a picture being shot by Gunnar Svan, Ai-ling's husband; and, as always with a Svan film, *Glitz* would give it big play. The actress had been summoned to a studio to pose for some of the pictures on display here. Others were from paparazzi, who found *Glitz* a lucrative market.

A paparazzo had caught the statuesque Beverly rising from a pool filled with lily pads, where she had fallen or had been thrown during a party at a famous Hollywood watering hole. The cameraman had managed to get on the roof, from which with his telephoto lens he had caught more than a few celebs in situations they would have rather he had not photographed. Beverly, drenched and looking stunned, was obviously screaming.

"Too much?" Ai-ling asked.

"*I* wouldn't," said Lloyd.

Ai-ling grinned. "File it. Maybe sometime."

Bill Lloyd was ten years her senior, and he was her mentor in print journalism. He was a bald man and wore gold-rimmed round glasses.

"How 'bout this?"

Ai-ling showed him another paparazzo shot, this one of Beverly Tree oozing her way out of a Lotus sports car, a maneuver that had shoved her skirt so high that her white panties showed. Her expression suggested that she was oblivious of what she was showing, probably because she'd had too much to drink. It was the kind of photo *Glitz* favored: mildly scandalous but not ruinous to the people pictured.

"We could do that one," said Lloyd.

Ai-ling smiled. "Our tastes match," she said.

That was not true. Bill Lloyd was her mentor in journalism, but he would never be her mentor about taste. Her esthetic judgment far surpassed his own. What was more, she had an instinct for what her target audience wanted. When she converted *Glitz* into a slick, upscale monthly, circulation had plummeted. Within a year, it had soared. If publication costs were not so high, it would be one of the most profitable magazines published in the United States.

"Look at this one," she said.

This photograph portrayed Beverly Tree standing before a buffet table at what was obviously an elegant garden party. Her dignity was fully intact. She was smiling on the late Richard Nixon—who, with eyes bulging and mouth half open, was staring into her cleavage.

"Go with it," said Lloyd.

Ai-ling shoved the color prints toward him, all but the rejected pile.

Here was where a fine line had to be drawn. The actress had posed nude, but *Glitz* did not publish nudity as, for example, *Playboy* would do, much, much less as *Penthouse* would do. Beverly Tree had posed because she trusted Ai-ling Cooper-Svan to display her nudity only in the most modest and graceful way.

"It's a responsibility," said Ai-ling.

Lloyd did not know if she meant a responsibility to the actress or one to her husband's film. She had money invested in *that,* of course, and was anxious to protect it. He suspected even so that Mrs. Cooper-Svan felt a genuine sensitivity about how the magazine would show off the actress. He could see on the "rejected" pile all the photos that showed even a shadow of pubic hair. The "accepted" photos were almost all rear views. The problem with the "possibles" was nipples. *Glitz* published many nudes but only a few that showed nipples.

Lloyd pushed one of the prints toward Ai-ling. Beverly Tree's right breast was clearly shown, but it was in profile, and the nipple was barely discernible.

Ai-ling nodded. "More than her public has ever seen of her, yet— I like it. Gunnar will like it."

Lloyd understood a distinction. Whether Gunnar liked the picture or not was immaterial. That Ai-ling judged he would like it was what counted.

Bill Lloyd was not the only person who thought the marriage between Ai-ling Cooper and Gunnar Svan was strange. It *was* strange.

He was a Swede, of course, the acclaimed director of low-budget art films, all full of woodsy-watery scenes with naked people cavorting around and doing nobody-was-sure-what to loud and soulful music. Ai-ling met him in Sweden, married him, and brought him to the States six years ago. She was his second wife. Since she brought him to Los Angeles he had directed four films, each a *succès d'estime,* none a commercial success. Ai-ling invested in each of these films. Her losses did not threaten to impoverish her, but they had been substantial. The word in the film colony was that Gunnar could not make films if Ai-ling did not subsidize him.

What was more, he was a tyrannical director who squabbled constantly with his actors. Rumor had it that he was a philanderer as well.

Bill Lloyd did not like the man at all. But Ai-ling did, apparently. She called him Top Gun, and the double entendre was deliberate.

"Settled, then," said Ai-ling. "Will you do the captions? I've got the draft."

2

Gunnar Svan stood with his legs spread wide apart, hands on hips, and glowered at the people assembled on his set in the Arizona desert.

"Gotterverdamn!" he shrieked. It wasn't German, it wasn't Swedish, and it wasn't English. It was Svanish, some people said. "Vy you could not unnershtand dee most simplest, dee most clarische instructions? Iss my Innglish so *difficult?* Iss you can't *oonderstand?*"

The sweating, dusty people standing around in the blazing sun would have told him, if they dared, that his English was not just difficult but impossible—not just because it was badly expressed but because it was so often meaningless. If he had spoken English like Dan Rather he would have been difficult to understand.

"Vunce again! Vunce again! Zeess pipples are not cowboyss und Indeentss! Zey are *real* pipples! Dey got 'motions. Dey got fillingss! Giff me—" He paused and grabbed up a paper cup filled with no-one-knew-what. He swallowed. "Drrrake! Giff me 'motions. Dese pipples not voodcarfed *nootcrackers!* You can *act?* Or not can act?"

"What the hell would you know about acting, you Svendisch con man?" asked Drake Rogers in a low voice. "I can act rings around you any day, you asshole." He raised his voice. "Whaddaya want, Gunnar?"

"Truth . . . Beauty!"

"Truth and beauty are waiting for him in his trailer," muttered Beverly Tree. "Beauty is, anyway. I saw Ron put a broad in the trailer half an hour ago. That's why he wants to get the scene shot, so he can hurry to the trailer and—"

"The *money,* folks," murmured John Doggs. "The money . . . Let us not forget why we are here."

The figure they all faced was something of an American icon. He was not very tall, but he was muscular and not in the least ashamed to show his body. That was a part of his self-created image, that he appeared on his outdoor sets without shirts, with an Hermés scarf tied around his neck to absorb his sweat. Where it was hot, he wore khaki safari shorts and bulky safari shoes, which were what he was wearing today. He was a fifty-years-later Cecil B. De-Mille, with a style everyone recognized, including those who did not in the least respect it.

He was a Swede. The remnants of his hair were yellow. The heavy hair on his chest and legs was almost invisible because it was so light. His eyes were pale blue.

What characterized him more than anything else was his furious pent-up energy. He was—some used the tired cliché—a coiled spring. No one denied that he exhausted himself. He threw himself into his work until the spring uncoiled and often left him limp.

Rogers looked at Doggs. " 'Tisn't *any money of his,*" he said.

"Whose money 'tis means nothing. He controls it. We get some of it because *he* releases it to us."

"Look at the bastard. Who the hell does he think he is, would somebody explain?"

"He thinks he's Ingmar Bergman."

"Well, he isn't."

"We tolerate him or walk off this set. To me, the money means more than the aggravation."

Drake Rogers yelled at Gunnar Svan. "What emotions, Gunnar? Exactly?"

"Zees ees what *you* are supposed to know, mine friend! You are zee actor! Vat vould a man feel in zee situation describe in zee screep'?"

"Nausea," yelled Rogers. "Toward anyone who'd write a script this bad."

"You haf contract to play eet. *Now play eet!* Gottverdammnt!"

Drake Rogers smiled on each of his fellow actors standing around him. " 'Play eet.' " He shook his head. "Okay, what's my next line? 'Those men are an excrescence.' Alright, let's play eet. Like 'nootcrackers.' "

Ingrid Karlsen watched the shooting of the scene from the broad window of the director's trailer. She sat on the couch, sipping from a light Scotch and soda, her eyes narrowed, studying the action.

Beverly Tree. God, what she would give to be Beverly Tree! Drake Rogers. If she were Beverly Tree, she would be kissed by Drake Rogers! She had the script open before her and knew he was going to kiss her in this scene.

Or he might, if Mr. Svan ever allowed them to get to that point. He was unhappy. She could not tell what he was saying, but she could hear enough to know that he was yelling. Ingrid wished she dared open the window and hear what Mr. Svan was telling his actors. She might hear something extremely valuable, some wonderful tip that would help her become a star.

Become a star— She was not naive. It wasn't just a matter of talent, or a matter of beauty; she might turn out to have talent, and certainly she was beautiful, in everybody's judgment; but Pam had explained it required something more. So, okay. She was ready.

Suddenly Mr. Svan threw his arms in the air and walked away from the cameras and crew, toward the trailer. Ingrid rushed into the kitchen and dumped her drink. She snatched a spray from her purse and sweetened her breath. She slapped at her hot-pink mini to smooth out any wrinkles she may have caused by lounging on the couch. She tugged down on her white polo shirt to stretch it more tightly over her breasts. She had only a second to run her hands down her long blond hair before the door opened and Gunnar Svan stalked into the trailer.

He slammed the door behind him. Then he noticed her. He glared at her. *"Who . . . ?"* Then the tension left his face. His eyes softened. "Oh, yes. Meess Karlsen. Yes. I vass expecting you. You are very beautiful, as was promised. Sit down. A durink, hmm?" He kicked off his shoes and pulled off his socks.

"If you are."

"Yes. Dzheen? Wodka? Scots?"

"A light Scotch, please."

Svan poured Scotch over ice and handed the glass to Ingrid. It was not a light drink. He mixed "dzheen" and vermouth to make himself a martini.

"It was kind of you to have me brought to your trailer. Actually, though, I would have liked to be out on the set, watching your actors work."

"Ahh! Ven I get actorss, I haf you dere to see dem act. Vat I got out dere iss galoots."

"Well . . . Then I could have watched *you* work."

Svan grinned. "You are like a zephyr, Mees Karlsen. How oldt are you?"

"I turned eighteen two weeks ago."

"And so beautiful. You are a true blondt, no?"

She lowered her eyes. "Yes."

He reached to a shelf behind his chair and picked up a script. He handed it across the coffee table, to Ingrid on the couch. "Eess a screep'," he said. "Love story. Very nice. Young pipples. Beautiful. Might be you could play."

Ingrid flushed. She knew she had come to read for him, but was he actually suggesting she could have a part in his next picture? She began to look through the pages. Glancing as quickly as she could, she saw only one role for a girl as young as she was, and it was the female lead. My god!

"Mees Karlsen. Must ask qvestion. You read screep', you see zee young girl, zee star of feelm, mus' appear in nude? You can do thees?"

Ingrid lifted her chin high, then closed her eyes and nodded.

"Goot. Goot. Look at page forrty-five. See zee talk between Jan und Anna? Zees I weesh you to read for me. I do zee Jan lines. I know dem. I write dees screep' mine zelf."

Ingrid flipped to the page and stared at the dialogue.

"Vee read, say, five page. Now, you notice zat in zees scene Anna ees nude. I vish you to read in zee nude. You must demonstrate to mee that you haff the courache, eef it require such, to act your role while you haff no clothes on. Take a swallow of your Scots, eef dat will calm you. Zen read zee five pages, to see what emotionss iss dere. Ven you feel confident, ve read."

Ingrid read the five pages of dialogue. She didn't understand the character, couldn't figure out what motivated her. But she was afraid to ask anything.

She sighed quietly and nodded. "You want me to—?" She gestured with her hands in front of her.

"Take off zee clothes," said Svan. "I know that Actors Eqvity says no do ziss, no nude auditions. But how I know a girl can act in nude eef I do not audition her in nude?"

"I suppose you couldn't," said Ingrid as she lifted her polo shirt.

TWO

WEDNESDAY, JULY 15

Frederick Fisher, Ai-ling's accountant, sat on the couch facing her desk. She had come from behind the desk and sat there with him.

"What are you telling me, Fisher? That Gunnar is stealing from me? I want the truth, and I want it flat out. Is Gunnar stealing from me?"

"I just show you the numbers, Mrs. Cooper-Svan. What they mean"—he shook his head—"I leave to you. I give you the numbers. You make the judgments."

"To hell with that, Fisher. You don't show me numbers, then refuse to tell me what they stand for. Am I being robbed? Am I?"

Frederick Fisher was a short, slight man with prominent ears and a prominent Adam's apple. He probably didn't weigh a hundred twenty pounds. He was pallid, and his beard showed through his skin.

"Well— Svan & Associates, Incorporated, list their fees paid to Dragon Brothers—"

"That's the fellow that handled the animals? All those goddamned animals he had to have?"

"Supplied the animals. And handled them. Svan & Associates show they paid Dragon Brothers $875,000 for their services on *Woodland Ecstasy*. In the ordinary course of an audit, you do inquire of some of the people to whom sums were paid out. Dragon Brothers say they billed for $715,000, and that is what they were paid."

"So what became of the $160,000? What did he do with it?"

"There wasn't any $160,000. Let me go on. I've found discrepancies of a little over a million dollars. Specifically"—he turned over a sheet of paper and pointed at a handwritten figure—"$1,061,354."

Ai-ling sighed and shook her head. " 'Discrepancy.' What's a discrepancy?"

"What's been going on is this. Svan & Associates contracted to pay Brad Linscott fifteen percent of the profits on the film—in addition, of course, to his fee. Not an unusual arrangement, you know."

"A heavy hitter. He was probably worth it. The picture didn't have a chance without him, anyway. I supposed if people didn't care all that much about Gunnar's art, at least they'd go to see Brad. He's got millions of loyal fans."

"Yes. Of course, he hasn't been paid a nickel from his profit-sharing deal. The story from Svan & Associates is that the film hasn't *made* a profit."

"I can attest to that," said Ai-ling wryly.

"Yes. Well, I found the million-whatever. But I am certain there's more. I can't prove it, but I suspect there have been kickbacks, too. In other words, Svan & Associates pay a million bucks to some contractor, and the contractor kicks back a hundred thousand."

"To whom?"

Frederick Fisher drew a deep breath, blew it out in an audible sigh, and shook his head. "To Mr. Svan. Nobody makes a profit but him."

"What's he got, a Swiss bank account?"

"The Swiss don't have those secret accounts anymore. But there are ways—"

"Son of a bitch! I put $11,000,000 in *Woodland Ecstasy*. When he told me it was losing money, I handed over another $3,500,000. And you're telling me the son of a bitch *didn't* lose money. I've been had!"

"You're not the only one. All of the investors. Anyone who had an equity interest."

Ai-ling crushed a cigarette in the ashtray on the small round table and lifted her margarita. She licked salt from the rim of the glass, then took a sip.

"La Sonrisa serves a good margarita," she said. "Not every bar does."

She and Lincoln Hilliard sat on a banquette facing a broad window that overlooked the Pacific in the distance and below. The curved banquette formed a sort of cubicle, intended to afford privacy to the people who sat there. Erring couples met at La Sonrisa for that very reason; they could sit and talk and drink and be seen by no one else in the bar.

The privacy allowed Ai-ling to indulge an eccentricity of hers: sitting with her legs spread wide apart, her elbow on her knee, her chin in her hand, usually showing a cynical, world-weary smile. Her skirt crept back, of course, showing her bare legs all the way to the triangle of the opaque black briefs she wore to guard her modesty. Her friends enjoyed this whimsical idiosyncrasy of Ai-ling's, but only her friends were ever allowed to see it; she was not an exhibitionist.

"Anyway, Link, I thought you ought to know. I'm not surprised entirely. I hope you're not."

Lincoln Hilliard was a broad-shouldered, heavyset man with a bit of gray beginning to appear in his close-trimmed hair and coarse grizzly beard. He had played college football but had received no offer from the pros, so went on to medical school and was now a psychiatrist. He was two or three years older than Ai-ling and had never concealed his disappointment that she had chosen to marry Gunnar Svan.

"I'm realistic," he said glumly. "Frankly, I expected to lose my investment. But, by god, I didn't expect to have it stolen from me!"

"I'm sorry I suggested you put money in anything of Gunnar's. I do it, but I have a different reason."

"Reasons aren't too different," said Lincoln. He put his hands on hers.

"You want to tell me, once again, what a wretched mistake I made?"

"Okay. You made a mistake. I've said it too many times. He's a poseur—"

"So was— So was Jack Kennedy. So was Ron Reagan. So was Franklin D. Roosevelt. Poses make *success,* Link. The world runs on images, not on reality. Top Gun has a little something going for him."

"Not little, I should imagine."

"You compare very favorably, lover."

"Why in god's name did you marry the bastard, Eileen? You knew I—"

She closed her hands around his. "There's an old saying, Link. 'Every man in his life should love a woman, write a book, and kill a man.' It's not the same for a woman. Every woman in her life is entitled to make one huge mistake. I suppose I brought him home as a trophy. I thought I was pretty smart: marrying a respected Swedish director."

"Do you think you have to pay for it for the rest of your life?"

"I don't have to pay for it the rest of this evening," she said. "Why don't we go in for dinner, then—" She grinned. "—I bet we can think of something."

Lincoln bent over and kissed her behind the ear. "I almost wish he'd find out."

"Wouldn't make any difference. He's sleeping with some chick tonight, in his trailer over in Arizona."

FRIDAY, JULY 17

The tall gray-haired woman who sat in the chair facing the glass desk was conspicuously impressed with her client. Ai-ling leaned forward over the desk, her elbows resting on it. Her legs were wide apart, and through the glass the woman could see legs and briefs. Ai-ling dragged hard on a cigarette.

"I got what you wanted," said the woman. She handed over a manila envelope imprinted—

MARGARET SIMMS & ASSOCIATES

Ai-ling poured a dozen five-by-seven black-and-white prints out of the envelope. "More than one," she said. "In the course of a week, he had—?"

"I'm afraid so. My man got pictures of three. There may be others."

Ai-ling put her finger on one of the photos. "Is this one Pamela Murphy?"

Margaret Simms nodded. "That's Pamela, née Murphy, aka Starr."

"Well, I must say she looks like what I'd expected. She looks like a stripteaser."

"She calls herself an 'exotic dancer,'" Margaret Simms said dryly.

"Is that the car he bought her? A BMW."

"That's the car."

"How old is she?"

"Twenty-six."

"And she takes off her clothes for a living," mused Ai-ling. "I guess that would appeal to Gunnar. He has a taste for that sort of thing." She picked up another picture, of a husky young woman. "Who's this one?"

"That's Muriel Paul. She works in a doughnut shop, midnight shift. Part-time hooker also. The vice squad tolerates her because she was an informant in an important case a couple of years ago, helped detectives break up a car-theft ring."

"He keeps nice company, doesn't he? Who's the third one?"

"Ingrid Karlsen. She's a wannabe actress. Dropped out of high school. For the past couple of weeks she's been living with him in the trailer in Arizona."

"How old is she?"

"She's seventeen."

"Is he giving *her* money?"

"Apparently not." Margaret Simms smiled. "I imagine he's giving her acting lessons."

"Okay," said Ai-ling grimly. "Let's drop it for now. I suppose you got my check. Give me a statement for what you've done since your last one."

TUESDAY, JULY 21

Ai-ling clamped her knees tight together as she confronted the man who stood at her desk.

"Sit down, Mr. Karlsen," she said. She pointed to the chair in front of her desk. "Please . . . sit down."

Piers Karlsen was an angry man. His anger was not threatening, but it was real. He was a big man. His face was red. The veins at his temples were swollen, and she could see them pulsing. He was also extraordinarily handsome. One of Ai-ling's thoughts was—why couldn't I have married *this* Swede instead of the one I got?

"I would appreciate it if you would say it all again. Tell me what you came here to tell me, one more time, please. Try to be a little more rational. I know you're angry, and maybe you have good reason to be, but I want to understand exactly what you're saying."

She swung her chair around and touched a button on a control panel on her credenza. It started a tape recorder. The microphones were in the ceiling and were very sensitive.

"I'm saying your husband is corrupting my daughter," said Karlsen.

" 'Corrupting'? Please?"

"Mrs. Svan— I told you. To put the matter in the bluntest words, your forty-year-old husband is fucking my seventeen-year-old daughter!"

"Why don't you call the police?"

"You don't believe me."

"No, I don't. Gunnar is no angel, but I don't think he is capable of seducing a seventeen-year-old girl. No . . . I don't think he's capable of that."

Piers Karlsen watched Ai-ling light a cigarette. Maybe he didn't notice that her hands trembled.

"Mrs. Svan, my wife and I brought Ingrid here from Sweden when she was three years old. Five years ago my wife died. For five years, I have been mother and father to Ingrid, as best I could. I own a small photofinishing shop and work long, long hours to make a living. I haven't been able to be what two parents should be. I know when she began to drink and to smoke marijuana. I knew when she began to see boys, older boys; and I doubt she has been a virgin since she was fourteen. I couldn't stop her. I couldn't govern her. But now— Now she is living with your husband in his trailer, on a motion-picture set in Arizona."

"Have you talked with her?"

"I found her. I talked to her. She says he has promised to make her the star of a picture he means to make, starting later this year. It is her dream. It is what she always wanted. Tell me, Mrs. Svan, will your husband really make my daughter a star?"

"If he does, is all forgiven?"

Piers Karlsen paused. "I want her to be what she wants," he said soberly.

Ai-ling leaned forward and rested her elbows on the

glass top of her desk. She allowed her legs to part. "We're not talking about virginity then, are we? We're not talking about corruption or seduction. We're talking about the girl getting what she's paying for. What is it you're asking me to do—rein in a straying husband or make him keep his promises to Ingrid?"

"Either one, Mrs. Svan," said Piers Karlsen, his voice hard and angry.

"Suppose I can't?"

"In that case, I might have to deal with the matter some other way."

Ai-ling turned around and switched off the recorder.

SATURDAY, JULY 25

Gunnar had come home. Shooting had been suspended for the weekend.

He and Ai-ling sat in the living room of their home on Loma Vista Drive. He had a martini in his right hand. He was sprawled in the corner of a leather couch, wearing safari shorts and a white polo shirt. As was customary with him, he was barefoot while indoors. He frowned thoughtfully as Ai-ling interrupted their conversation while she lit still another Marlboro.

He was doing something that he knew made her very nervous. He had removed a thousand-year-old jade Buddha from the glass case in which it was displayed and was fingering it—fondling it, actually. It was worth more than the house. She had inherited it from her grandmother. He didn't take it out and handle it to distress Ai-ling; he was drawn to the eight-inch figurine and almost shared the Chinese superstition that jade was life giving.

She was wearing a loose white dress with a short skirt and deep, wide cleavage. She sat with her legs spread, black tights showing, and as she leaned forward her breasts seemed about to fall out of the dress at any moment.

"Anyway, I'm surprised you came home," she said. "I thought you were having a good time in Arizona."

"I hear sarcastical," said Gunnar. "Ai-ling . . . Why sarcastical?"

Gunnar had always called her Ai-ling, never Eileen. She had appreciated that until she realized that he believed the Chinese were an inferior race and that she, with her Chinese ancestry, was his inferior. He called her Ai-ling to put her down.

"You must have had a scheduling problem at times. Of course, you *would* know when the beauteous Pamela was coming. She wouldn't come on nights when she was working. Nor, I suppose, would Muriel. But where on earth did you hide Ingrid when one of those was coming?"

"Vun uff my galoot actorss must have called and said naughty zings."

"Do you know how old Ingrid is?"

"Who iss Ingrid?"

"Don't play around, Gunnar. Ingrid Karlsen has been living with you in your director's trailer for three weeks. And she's just seventeen."

Gunnar stiffened and swelled with a deep breath. He lifted his glass and tossed back the rest of his martini. "She liffs wiz me no more," he said. "Her fadder comes and takes her. She tolds me she iss *eighteen*. He says seventeen."

"You're lucky he didn't kill you."

"He spokes of zat possibles."

"Do you have any idea what kind of risks you're taking? If you have that girl pregnant, her father killing you might be the least that could happen to you. Besides that—"

"Vat iss besides dat?" he asked. He got up and strode purposefully to the bar to mix himself another drink.

"Well, let me put it to you this way, Gunnar. If you think you're going to sleep with me tonight, get real. You've been dicking a stripteaser—and bought her a car. Do you suppose you're the only man in her life? She gets around, Gunnar. And god knows what else she gets, besides around. But worse than that— Do you want to pretend you don't know your girlfriend Muriel is a part-time hooker? She turns tricks on Sunset Boulevard. The microbiology she may carry around staggers the imagination. If you've passed an infection to that seventeen-year-old girl, you're in *very* big trouble. You're not going to get the chance to pass it to me."

"Oh? Iss dee marritch den *terminate,* Ai-ling?"

"That depends on how much you clean up your act. I've got a lot invested in you. Besides money, there's reputation—"

"Und eee-gaw."

"Yes, ego. You've made a fool of me."

"Vas eessy," he said.

MONDAY, JULY 27

Ai-ling sat again with Lincoln Hilliard, on the same banquette in La Sonrisa where they had met twelve days before.

"I'm going to kill him, Link," she said in a calm, matter-of-fact tone. "Will you help me?"

Lincoln grinned and chuckled. "You must feel like it," he said. "And I can't say I blame you. I'm not too fond of him myself."

"I'm serious."

Lincoln's grin disappeared. "C'mon, Eileen. You don't dare even think about it."

"Well, think about this. Gunnar Svan is my *construct*. I made him what he is. Well— I made him an American film director. He had a certain cult following when he was working in Sweden, and I thought he had a special talent—"

"He does. He's a fine director."

"He wouldn't be, without me. No one would hire him. His pictures don't make money."

"Or maybe they do."

She nodded. She put her cigarette aside and picked up her margarita. "Maybe they do. When the audit is all finished, we'll know. But that's not all I've got against him. Link, the man is cheating on me! And not just a little bit, either. You know I call him Top Gun, and you know why. I'm not going to suggest I wasn't attracted by his prowess and didn't appreciate it. I never guessed how much he'd want to spread it around."

Link shrugged. "Well. After all, we—"

"Not the same," she snapped. "You and I . . . You love me. You've told me so. I care for you, too. So we sleep together now and then. But Gunnar sleeps *around!* With sluts! He bought a $60,000 car for a *stripteaser!* He messes around with a hooker. And his latest conquest is a seventeen-year-old girl! I won't let him touch me anymore. He may be carrying a disease. The marriage is over, and he's citing the California community property law to me."

"Even so, you don't dare kill him," said Link gravely. "You mustn't even think about it."

"Give me one good reason."

"You'll get caught."

Ai-ling dragged on her cigarette. She stiffened her back and sat erect. "Give me credit, Link. I'm not stupid. I can do it so no one will *ever* figure it out."

"Don't try it, Eileen. There's no such thing as a perfect murder."

She grinned. "No? Look at the statistics. Ask LAPD how many case files remain open. You won't help me, huh?"

"I'll help you in one way," he said. "I have just forgotten that we ever had this conversation."

Ai-ling reached for his hand. "After a decent period of mourning, I'll marry you, Link. As my husband, you won't be able to testify against me."

THREE

THURSDAY, JULY 30—6:12 P.M.

Gunnar sat in the living room, dressed as he had been last Saturday: his favorite khaki shorts, a white polo shirt, and barefoot. The time was a little after six in the evening, and he was drinking his third martini.

Ai-ling handed him a fourth one. "I suppose we might as well be civil," she said. "A little drink or two helps."

She didn't make margaritas at home. But she drank tequila on the rocks, sometimes with a slice of lime. When she was at the bar mixing his fourth martini, she poured half of her second tequila into the sink. As she handed him the martini, she had what looked like her own third fresh drink.

"Vy not?" he muttered. "Dank you, Ai-ling. You can be a goot girl ven you vant to."

They'd had their first drinks on the stone terrace and had come inside the air-conditioned house to escape the heat. Ai-ling was wearing a white tennis dress, though she hadn't been playing tennis.

"Have you heard anything more from the Karlsens? I mean—"

Gunnar shook his head.

"You can pacify the man by giving the girl a part in a picture," she said.

"I all but promised her dee starring role in dat screep' I write. She reads for me. She kent act. She all— How you say? Vooden."

"I never noticed that Beverly Tree can act, either. That doesn't seem to have impeded—" She decided not to suggest that he probably slept with her, too.

"Uff course . . . Uff course, eef you vould geef Ingrid dee beeg beeldup een *Gleetz*—"

"Sure."

"A goot story. A preetty leetle Svedish girl, an eemigrant, vots mutter hass died. Gunnar Svan discoverss great talent. Peectures. No nudes. Leetle girl too modest for dat. Maybe show in oondervear: vite bra und pawnties. Den, een feelm leetle girl iss nude, uff course. Story say how deefeecult to persvade her. Hmm?"

Ai-ling shrugged. "Why not? We have *Glitz*. Why not use it? Maybe a Gunnar Svan film can make money for once. Neither of us would mind that."

"Uhmm," he murmured. He finished his third martini and picked up the fourth one she had brought him. "Dot vould be alright. You'll do diss, Ai-ling? It satisfy dat big dummy her fadder."

The maid usually stayed to prepare dinner. Once she served it, she was free for the day. Ai-ling would clear the table. This afternoon Ai-ling had told her Mr. Svan was going to be late so she should make something that could be heated in the microwave and go on home at five o'clock. The woman had left a salad in the refrigerator and a lasagna in the microwave.

Ai-ling went to the kitchen, started the microwave, and carried the salad to the dining table, which was already set with dishes and silverware. Back in the kitchen, she opened a bottle of Chianti. She started the coffeemaker.

"Hungry?"

Gunnar had smelled the lasagna. "Yiss," he said. "Smill goot."

She served him and poured him a glass of wine. "Personally, I couldn't eat lasagna without Chianti," she said. "It's good for the digestion, too."

He nodded. "I thinking. Vat if ve run two story? First say Ingrid too modest to be nude. Second have frames from peecture, showing her *absolute* nude."

"Are you going to call Piers Karlsen and tell him his daughter gets the part?"

Gunnar frowned. "Maybe better someone else do thees. He vass very angry, very threatening man."

"Do you want *me* to call him?"

"Vould be pair-feect! I 'preciate it, Ai-ling. You an' me, ve can vork partners, no?"

Ai-ling raised her glass. "We can work partners, yes. Why not?"

She kept his wineglass full. He ate hungrily and drank four glasses of wine. Then she poured coffee and cognac. When Gunnar left the table he staggered. He went in his den, sat down in his recliner chair, and used the clicker to switch on the television. He clicked several more times, channel-surfing. Within five minutes Ai-ling could hear him snoring.

She had bought a new bath towel. She tossed it on the floor behind his chair.

She went to the cellar. Their—actually, *her*—house was old, having been built in 1933 by the ill-starred couple Joseph and Ida Linden, whose careers as co-stars, first of silent films, then of talkies, came to a sudden end when their gruesomely murdered bodies were found in the cellar to which Ai-ling now descended. She knew where the bodies had been found: in what was now the laundry room. For decades owners of the house had kept the room virtually sealed and had never entered it. When she bought the house, fifteen years ago, she had ordered the room made into a laundry. A problem with it, as with the other rooms in the cellar, was that the floor was not level. When the washing machine was a little unbalanced and in its spin cycle, it "walked." She was replacing the machine, and this time she had ordered holes drilled in the floor and two-by-fours bolted to the concrete to lock the washer between them and keep it from moving.

Exploring the house she had noticed a star drill lying on the laundry-room floor. A star drill was a steel bar some sixteen inches long, with a shaped bit on one end. Set on the floor and pounded with a heavy hammer, it could drill a hole in concrete or soft stone. The workman hit it, turned it, and hit it and turned it again and again. It was a noisy process and kicked up much dust, but the contractor explained that the noise and dust were far less than a pneumatic drill would make. The star drill was suitable for pounding in the six holes. When the holes were drilled, each some six inches deep, lead anchors would be driven into them, and the coarse threads on heavy screws would bite into the lead, expand it, and fasten the two-by-fours securely in place.

Ai-ling had made her plan, as she had promised Link Hilliard. She had a pair of disposable plastic kitchen gloves with her. She put them on, picked up the star drill, whacked the floor a couple of times to knock the concrete dust off it, and went upstairs.

As she reached the top of the cellar stairs the telephone rang. Damn! It would wake Gunnar! He had a phone on the table beside his recliner. He— It stopped after three rings. He had answered it!

She put down the star drill and walked into the living room, to the door to the den. He was talking on the phone. "Ya, ya, ya," she heard him say. He slurred his words. "Ya. Ve do it tomorrow."

She watched him. He stared at the television and shook his head, as if he were disoriented. He ought to be; he'd drunk enough. She waited. His chin fell. He jerked it up. It fell again. He grunted, then surrendered. Within two minutes he was sound asleep again.

She returned to the kitchen for the star drill. When she came back, he was snoring lightly. She put the star drill down on the bath towel.

Now she took off her clothes, all of them, and when she was quite naked she picked up the star drill with her gloved hands. She stepped around, between the television set and the recliner, facing the slumbering Gunnar.

"Gunnar. Gunnar! Wake up!"

He lifted his head laboriously. His torpid, heavy-lidded eyes did not focus on her. "Vat you vant, Ai-ling? Vat you vant right now?"

"You dirty son of a bitch," she growled.

She raised the star drill high and brought it down on his

head. Through the hard metal she could feel the heavy bar crack his skull and drive fragments of bone into his brain. It was the most sickening feeling she had ever known, and the lasagna rose in her throat. As she had expected, blood flew. That was why she was naked, so that none of his blood would be found on anything she had worn. She looked at herself in horror. His blood ran down her breasts and belly.

She gathered strength and determination, raised the steel bar, and struck a second time. This time, more blood flew. Gasping for breath, she lifted the bar above her head in both hands and crashed it down a third time.

Dizzy with nausea, hyperventilating, she stared at her bloody body and legs. *God, murder was not easy!*

But neither would be the penalty for murder. She fought for control, got it, and reached for the towel. She rubbed herself with it, bloodying the towel but clearing her skin of all but stains of blood.

Carrying the towel, she ran up the stairs to the bathroom of the master bedroom suite. She got in the shower and turned on the water. Not even waiting for the water to become warm, Ai-ling stood in the stream and watched the last traces of blood wash down the drain. She got out of the shower and dried herself. She left the water running, so that every possible trace of blood would go through the pipes and out of the house. She left the bloody towel in the shower, to be drenched with water while she did her other work.

Downstairs, she pulled on the plastic gloves again.

She looked at the digital clock on the microwave. It was 7:14. She had to move.

Still naked, she rushed back to the den, where the body of Gunnar, drenched in blood, slumped in his recliner. She grabbed up the star drill, took it to the kitchen, and rinsed the blood off it—again letting the water run in the sink until every traceable drop of blood had gone down the drain.

She dried the drill with paper towels and returned it to the laundry room.

Back in the kitchen she put the paper towels and the plastic gloves in the garbage disposal and set it running. To be sure every fragment went through the disposal, she dropped six small potatoes and a handful of ice cubes into the disposal and let them serve to scrub the insides of the machine.

She had thought through everything.

She picked up her tennis whites and hurried upstairs. In her bedroom she sat down on the bed and punched a number into the telephone.

"Piers?"

"Yes."

"Brenda."

"Uhh . . ."

"I called you at your shop this afternoon. You said you might be interested. I've been thinking about you ever since. You haven't figured out who I am, have you?"

"No, I—"

Ai-ling laughed a small, tinkly laugh. She had practiced it. "You'll know me when you see me. I've caught it over the counter that you think I'm interesting. Men can't conceal that."

"I hope I've not been—"

"A woman can take it as she wants, Piers. I've taken it as a compliment, and I decided we might experiment with a more personal relationship. I mean, we might if you are interested. Only if you are interested."

"Well, yes."

"Great! How about the corner of Wilshire and Western. You know where that is?"

"I know . . . Brenda."

"Okay. It's gonna take me, like, half an hour, or like that. Why don't you park your car someplace and wait for me? Say northwest corner. I drive a white Pontiac convertible. We'll go someplace. Unless you surprise me, we'll have a hell of a good time, Piers."

She heard his breath. "I'll be there."

7:22 P.M.

There were still more things to do. She pulled on her tennis whites again.

She went to the living room. Sitting on an ornate table was the glass case that displayed the jade Buddha. She picked up a table lamp and threw it at the case. The glass shattered, and she lifted out the Buddha.

She went to the kitchen, to the back door. She wrapped a towel around a cleaver and punched out the lower left pane of glass. She opened the door and, using a Kleenex, picked up the shards of glass and tossed them on the kitchen floor. She left the door unlocked.

She hurried upstairs and took the bath towel from the still-running shower. She wrung it out, put it under the shower stream again, then wrung it out again. She carried it to the cellar and put it in the dryer.

Standing in the kitchen, she reviewed everything she had done. She had thought about this plan for a week— and intently since Monday. She would trust Link with the

Buddha, to hold it for her until they decided what they could do with it—probably pound it to dust and scatter it, unhappily. For the moment she would hide it under the spare tire in her car.

8:08 P.M.

"I am *so* sorry to be so late," Ai-ling said to Adrienne Boswell. "I— There's no excuse for it."

Adrienne was sitting at a table at Umberto's. She smiled and shrugged. "I haven't suffered," she said, nodding at the drink on the table. "It's part of my game, waiting for people. Sometimes it's not a pleasure. Sometimes it is. You can keep me waiting at Umberto's any time you want."

Ai-ling had never met Adrienne Boswell before but would have known her even if the captain had not said she was waiting at Mrs. Cooper-Svan's table. Adrienne was a very well-known independent journalist and had written three intimate interviews that *Glitz* had published. She was an exceptionally attractive woman with green eyes and red hair, wearing a spectacularly short green minidress. She was Ai-ling's age, exactly. Ai-ling admired the fact that Adrienne had attained her name and success without the advantage of an inheritance.

"Well . . . I wish I could have published your pieces on the Jimmy Hoffa matter," said Ai-ling.

Adrienne smiled. "Considering what you pay, I wish you could have, too."

Ai-ling returned her smile. "You didn't offer them."

"I didn't think they really suited you."

"I understand. In future, let *me* make that judgment, will you?"

Adrienne nodded.

"I certainly don't suggest you come to my staff," said Ai-ling. "You're an independent, and it's true that some of your best stuff wouldn't do in *Glitz*. I have a feeling, though, that we can be mutually productive. I'm thinking of something big. I'll do a favor for you, and you do one for me. We could start a partnership that can be good for both of us."

"What do you have in mind, Mrs. Cooper-Svan?"

"To begin with, can we drop the 'Miss' and 'Mrs.' bit? I'm Ai-ling. People who really know me call me Ai-ling, not Eileen. If I guess correctly, you checked me out thoroughly before you agreed to meet me."

Adrienne smiled. "As you did me."

"Alright. Let's start with the favor I'll do for you. There's a hell of a lot of gossip around town about Gunnar and me. I'll give you an exclusive. I'll tell you the whole damned story. We can't run that in *Glitz*. You might be able to sell it to *Vanity Fair*. Or wherever. I assume you will give me a break, not turn me into some kind of grotesque marionette. Or Gunnar either. It can be worked. Don't you think?"

"That's the favor you do me," said Adrienne. "What favor do I do you?"

"I brought something for you to see," said Ai-ling. She opened a small leather briefcase and handed over the layout of the story, with pictures, of Beverly Tree. "Look at the photos."

Adrienne nodded. "Yes. Beautiful. Uh . . . tasteful. Showing enough to— But not too much."

"I work hard at that . . . being tasteful. That photo spread is not going to hurt Beverly at all. To the contrary.

So— How about a respectful article on the acclaimed investigative journalist Adrienne Boswell—illustrated with equally artistic and tasteful pictures?"

Adrienne covered her eyes with one hand. "Oh, my god! You can't be serious!"

"Why not? You are a Los Angeles celebrity—and deserve to be. You are widely admired. A beautiful photo spread in *Glitz*, with carefully written text about your life and achievements, can't possibly hurt you—but will do you immense good instead. It's a career move."

Adrienne laughed. "It will end my relationship with my very special friend, Dan."

"If so, is he worth having?" asked Ai-ling bluntly. "I am married to an old-world man with definitive ideas about what I should be. I don't let him run my life. Does your boyfriend run yours?"

"Well, I do love him."

"I love Gunnar. But if I thought I could improve the circulation of *Glitz* a million copies a month by appearing in its pages looking like a *Penthouse* 'Pet,' I would do it. I'm a *woman,* Adrienne. Have you read anything of Betty Dodson's?"

"As a matter of fact, I have."

"Then—?"

Adrienne raised her chin high. "Will you give me approval of the pictures you choose to publish?"

"Yes, and you will be the first woman ever to have that veto."

"Alright. Agreed. Now, this interview."

"Start now," said Ai-ling.

Adrienne noticed tension in Ai-ling but attributed it to the no-smoking rule that now prevailed in Los Angeles restaurants. She snapped her finger to summon a waiter to bring Ai-ling a drink. When the waiter had taken the order for a margarita, Adrienne asked, "What, exactly, does go on between you and a husband who has a reputation for getting into the pants of every woman who comes near him?"

"That's exaggerated," said Ai-ling. "Gunnar's a strong, virile man. I'm sure he— Well . . . If I can stand his occasional adventure, the world should."

"The story is around that one of his adventures is with an 'exotic dancer.' "

"That kind of thing intrigues European men."

"Are you saying there's no difficulty between you and Gunnar?"

"No way. But name me a married couple that doesn't have difficulties. Gunnar drinks too much. He spends more than his movies make. But, Adrienne, the man is an *artist*. He's entitled to a few idiosyncrasies."

"Do you have your own?"

"If you're asking if I see another man, the answer is yes. If you're asking if I'm promiscuous, the answer is no. This is going to be an intriguing interview, isn't it? Can we handle it?"

Adrienne nodded and smiled. "I am sure we can."

10:21 P.M.

Ai-ling pulled her Jaguar close to the garage door and used the radio controller to open the door. A sensor had turned on bright lights all over the property as soon as she pulled into the driveway. She drove into the garage and used the controller to close the door. She had a permit to carry a pistol and had a tiny Baby Browning automatic in her hand as she left the car.

She went in the house.

She went to the den first. Gunnar's body was where she had left it. My god! A fly buzzed around it, feeding on his blood, and she all but retched. She stood there for a moment, then gagged herself with a finger and let herself vomit. A little of that on the floor would lend a further element of verisimilitude to the story she had to tell the police.

She went to the cellar. The dryer had stopped. The towel she had used to clean the blood from herself was dry. She folded it and carried it upstairs, to store it in a hall closet.

At 10:27 she punched in 911.

FOUR

Columbo did not regard himself at all as an *arbiter* *elegantiarum,* that is, an authority on what was elegant or in good taste. But as he squinted at the floodlit house where he was about to begin another murder investigation, he thought he saw something special. He had been inside many beautiful and luxurious homes, but he saw here a restrained elegance that impressed him. He couldn't define it, but he had seen many houses of rich and famous people, and they impressed him differently. This one impressed him as something different and special.

The house was not new. Oh, it was sixty years old, anyway. It had been a country house once. It was the kind of thing the old movie people built a long time ago, based on an idea of Spanish architecture or Mexican architecture: white stucco with a red-tiled roof, a small balcony enclosed in wrought iron above the front door. Pines. Junipers. All modest as compared to the gaudy, oversized houses people had been putting up since. He liked to speculate, and he guessed that the people who built this house had not been confident they would always have money; so they had built comfortable and beautiful, yet with restraint. Or— Or so he guessed; he really didn't know anything about stuff like this; it wasn't his field of expertise.

The street and driveway were crowded with police and emergency vehicles, some with their engines running and their red and blue lights blinking. Some reporters had already arrived, and a van with a dish antenna on top was sending a television signal to a station.

A man with a mini-cam trotted out ahead of Columbo and focused on him as he walked toward the house. The cameraman recognized the homicide detective with the flapping, tattered raincoat, the tousled hair, and the necktie tied so the narrow end hung below the wide end.

"Lieutenant Columbo! Got a statement for us? Anything to tell us?"

Columbo half frowned, half grinned, and turned up the palms of his hands. He'd been sent to look into a murder. They hadn't even told him who the victim was. He didn't tell the cameraman that, just grinned and walked on.

"Hiya, Sullivan," he said to the uniformed officer who stood guard at the front door. "Who got dead?"

"The victim's name is Gunnar Svan, Lieutenant. He's— *was*—a movie director. It's a hell of a bloody mess in there, Lieutenant. I've seen a lot, but— You may want somethin' for your stomach."

Columbo nodded. "Who's inside?"

"Sergeant Zimmer, plus another detective whose name I didn't catch. Also, the watch commander and Sergeant Alexander."

"Good group. I don't know why they called me. I won't have a thing to do. Keep an eye on my car for me, Sullivan, will ya?"

Sullivan stared skeptically at the lieutenant's scarred old Peugeot. "I don't think anybody will steal it, Sir. I mean, I don't think any car thief would—"

"For parts, Sullivan. For parts. You can't get parts for that kind of car anymore."

"Is there much demand for them?"

"For people who know how to appreciate 'em. Y' see, that car's a French car. You wouldn't believe how many miles I've got on it."

"How many, Lieutenant?"

"I don't really know, Sullivan. The speedometer quit a long time ago. It said eighty-nine thousand when I bought it, but I don't know if that was the first time around or the second or third. Anyway—"

"I'll keep an eye on it."

Detective Sergeant Martha Zimmer opened the door and came out. "Hey, Columbo," she said. "Haven't seen you for a while."

"Mrs. Columbo talked me into takin' a vacation. Three weeks in Hawaii. She had a grand time, but why anybody'd ever go there is more than I can figure. All I got out of it was a sunburn. 'Course, they do feed good, lots of fine seafood, and you know me, how I like anything that comes from the ocean. But lotsa pineapples . . . You can't even get a beer that hasn't got a chunk of pineapple in it."

"Well . . . come on in. And don't be thinkin' about pineapples when you get a look at this one."

Sergeant Martha Zimmer was a short, plump woman in her early thirties. Her dark hair was short, her apple-cheeked face was plump, and she wore no makeup. She was wearing a navy blue blazer over a white blouse, and gray slacks. Her badge hung from a leather folder tucked into her breast pocket. Her sidearm, a 9-mm Beretta, was visible in her left armpit. Columbo had worked with her more than once and knew she was a competent homicide detective. He was glad Martha Zimmer had caught this case.

"That's the victim's wife and her shrink," she said quietly, nodding toward a woman sitting on a couch in the living room. "After she called 911 she called her psychiatrist, and he came just after the first officers arrived."

"Well . . . figures. No family?"

"No kids. Nobody in the LA area, as far as I can figure. So, the shrink. His name is Dr. Hilliard. I'll introduce you. She's the publisher of *Glitz* magazine, incidentally."

"Mrs. Columbo looks at it sometimes. I don't. Not exactly my kind of thing."

They went from the foyer into the living room.

"Mrs. Cooper-Svan, this is Lieutenant Columbo, LAPD Homicide. He'll be in charge of the investigation."

Ai-ling nodded at Columbo. She didn't say anything. She sucked on a cigarette and stared at the wall. She had a bottle of tequila and a bucket of ice on the coffee table. She and Dr. Hilliard were sharing the bottle, apparently. And apparently she'd had a good deal to drink. Couldn't blame her. What would a woman drink who came home and found her husband—?

"My sympathy, Ma'am," said Columbo. "We'll try to be as, uh . . . *unobtrusive* as possible."

Ai-ling nodded again.

Martha nodded toward a lamp lying on the floor and the shattered remains of what apparently had been a glass display case. "Missing," she whispered to Columbo when they were out of Ai-ling's hearing. "One jade figurine from China, worth maybe a million."

Martha Zimmer led Columbo into the den. Sullivan had been right; it was a messy murder. The cause of death glared at everyone in the room—a crushed skull. Although it was of course not true, the room looked as if every ounce of blood in the victim's body had gushed from the gaping wound on his head.

He remained slumped forward in his reclining chair. Drying blood colored a white shirt so much it was all but impossible to see it had been white, a pair of khaki shorts only a little less. His bare feet were bloody, as was the chair. The floor was sticky with blood. Great drops of it were on the books in the bookcase at his side and on the magazines on a round table.

Columbo looked, then turned away; he was not beyond getting sick.

"You won't be bothered long with this one, Columbo," said a uniformed lieutenant—the watch commander. "Nothing much mysterious about it."

"Hiya, Lou," said Columbo—"Lou" meaning lieutenant. "Lessee . . . Lawrence, isn't it?"

"Pat Lawrence," said the lieutenant, extending his hand. "Glass broken in the back door. The widow says an extremely valuable antique is missing. Robbery."

"And murder," said Columbo. "That's how the man in the chair got dead."

"Right. That's why you're here. But it is pretty simple. Somebody broke in, killed him, and stole a jade Buddha worth ten fortunes."

Columbo turned down the corners of his mouth. He fished in his raincoat pocket and pulled out a cigar. "Gotta light?"

Lieutenant Lawrence snapped a lighter. "I mean . . . don't ya agree?" The uniformed lieutenant was in his forties from the look of him: a well-put-together man who probably had his uniforms tailored to fit him perfectly. He had a flushed face and blue eyes, and Columbo guessed he kept his cap on to hide receding hair.

"Well, I do have a question or two," said Columbo.

"Like?"

"Well . . . Somebody broke in, killed the victim, then stole this antique, then left. That leaves a very big question, don't ya think? *Who?*"

Dr. Harold Culp arrived. He took five minutes to examine the body, then stood erect and shrugged. "Pretty goddamned vicious," he said.

"How long's he been dead, Doc?" Columbo asked.

"You always ask."

"I gotta know."

"In a preliminary way, I'd say he died between seven and nine. How many times do I have to tell you that estimating time of death is not an exact science? But I'll go with between seven and nine."

"Anything but what's obvious?"

"What's not obvious is what I'll find out when I do the autopsy."

Columbo stared at the broken lock of the safe. "Martha. You always take notes. I . . . I got a pencil here somewhere, but—"

"I'll take the notes, Columbo."

"Right."

Lieutenant Lawrence spoke. "Crime Scene has looked at the entry point. Interested in that?"

"Lou, I'm interested in all of it."

They went to the back door. Shards of glass lay on the kitchen floor.

"How the perp got in, apparently," said Lawrence. "Broke one pane and reached through to turn the knob."

"Been dusted?" Columbo asked the Crime Scene technicians.

"Yes, Sir. No prints," said a young woman in a white blouse and dark-blue slacks. She wore a badge on her blouse and a nameplate that read PAVLOV.

"Any reason we can't open the door, then?"

She shook her head.

He opened the door and stepped out onto a narrow porch. Security lights blazed all around the house and on the swimming pool.

"Neighbors' houses are far enough away that—" Columbo went down two steps and ventured out into the yard. "Hey, guys. Who's got a flashlight?"

Lieutenant Lawrence had one, in a case on his belt. He handed it to Columbo, and Columbo bent over and used the beam of light to supplement the security floods. He walked around, bent over, staring at the bright spot of light he was guiding.

"Looka here," he said. He held the beam of light on a crescent-shaped bit of broken glass. "Hey, Crime Scene. Check this for prints and put it in an envelope as evidence. See if the pieces fit together at all."

"What would a piece of glass from that window be doing out here?" Martha Zimmer asked.

"I think that's a pretty good question, Martha."

"I mean, if the perp hit the window from outside, the glass would fall inside—or straight down, anyway."

"That right, Pavlov?" Columbo asked the young woman from the Crime Scene unit, who had already called out a photographer to make a picture of the shard of glass, show-ing where it lay just beyond the stoop, maybe four feet from the door.

"Yes, Sir," she said. "Our people have broken a lot of glass to demonstrate that."

Columbo grinned. "Did it before you were born."

Miss Pavlov looked as if she were in her mid-twenties. She was an attractive young woman with a pretty face and light-brown hair, one of the technicians the Department was hiring in ever greater numbers.

"Yes, Sir."

Columbo went back inside the house. He sat down at the kitchen table. Martha sat beside him, and Lieutenant Lawrence sat across the table.

"I guess the case isn't as simple as it looked," said Lawrence. "You've got questions, don't you, Columbo?"

"A few," said Columbo. "Let's figure what we're sup-posed to figure. The victim is sitting in his den watching TV. Somebody smashes a window in the kitchen door, comes through the kitchen door, and kills him with a 'blunt instrument.' Some way he doesn't hear the glass break, doesn't hear the killer coming. The killer beats him to death—and, guys, that's a savage beating. Victim doesn't resist but just sits there and takes it."

"After the first whack, he wouldn't have moved," said Martha.

"True." Columbo frowned over his cigar. It had gone out. Lieutenant Lawrence offered his lighter again. "What we got on this floor?" Columbo asked. "Living room, dining room, kitchen, pantry, den, foyer. Right?"

"Right," said Lieutenant Lawrence. "Upstairs there's a master bedroom suite and three more bedrooms and two more baths."

Columbo pointed to a door. "Where's that go? Basement?"

Pavlov answered. "Yes, Sir. There's an unfinished basement down there."

"What's that dust on the floor?" Columbo asked.

"I'm afraid one of our people tracked that up," said Pavlov. "Could've been me. They've been pounding holes in the concrete floor down there, with a star drill. Makes a lot of dust."

"What's a star drill?" asked Lieutenant Lawrence.

"It's a steel bar with a star-shaped pointy tip. They come in various sizes. They drill holes in concrete by pounding on them with a heavy hammer."

Lawrence grinned. "You're a walking encyclopedia, Pavlov."

"One was used as a murder weapon about a year ago," she said. "A man's head was beaten in with it."

"Y' don't say!" Columbo said. "A star drill. Let's see this thing."

Miss Pavlov led him down to the cellar and to the laundry room. The star drill lay on the dusty floor. Beside it was the heavy hammer, also a couple of big lead screw anchors and a two-by-four about a yard long. A second two-by-four was already fastened to the concrete floor.

Columbo puffed on his cigar. "Let's check your powers of observation, Pavlov. What's wrong with this scene?"

The young woman nodded. "I see it. There's no dust on the star drill. There's dust on everything else but none on the star drill."

"Exactly. I don't think you'll find any prints on that. That steel's too rough to take 'em. But have it checked. And take the star drill as a possible murder weapon."

3

Columbo squeezed his cigar to be sure there was no fire in it and stuck the cold butt in his raincoat pocket before he went in the living room to talk to Ai-ling. A cigar wouldn't offend her, though, probably, since she was slowly filling an ashtray with cigarette butts.

"I won't bother ya tonight, Ma'am," Columbo said to Ai-ling. "I will have to ask you some questions sooner or later. Maybe tomorrow."

"Ask them now, Lieutenant. You might as well. I'm not going to sleep tonight."

"Well— Where were you when this happened?"

"I was at dinner in a restaurant called Umberto's with a freelance writer named Adrienne Boswell. I arrived there about eight and left a few minutes before ten."

"Adrienne Boswell!"

Ai-ling managed a faint smile. "I suppose you know her, Lieutenant. She wrote a series of articles about the Regina-Hoffa murders."

Columbo nodded. "I know Adrienne very well. She plays a wicked game of pool. Uh— This statuette that was taken. It was worth—?"

"It was insured for a million dollars."

"Motive enough for killing a man," said Lincoln Hilliard grimly.

"Yes. Somebody had to know it was here. But Ma'am, with a valuable thing like that in the house, didn't you have an alarm system?"

"It wasn't turned on. Gunnar was here. When we were at home, we didn't turn it on."

"You left the house about—?"

"About seven-thirty. It takes roughly half an hour to drive to Umberto's."

"When you left, what was he doing?"

"The autopsy is going to tell you this, Lieutenant, so I may as well tell you now that Gunnar was drunk out of his mind. He was sitting there in his recliner chair, with the television set on, but I imagine he was asleep. Torpid might be a better word."

"Which would explain how someone could come up behind him and hit him," said Link Hilliard.

"Right. Well, I won't bother you anymore tonight. I— Oh, say, I do have one more little question. Kind of thing that comes up in the night and makes me lose sleep. Was that glass case some way locked or sealed? I mean, to steal the Buddha, did someone have to smash the case?"

"No. All you had to do was lift the top off. Why somebody smashed it is beyond me."

"Well, thank ya. I won't bother you anymore tonight. And, once again, my sympathies, Mrs. Svan."

Columbo returned to the den and and looked around one more time. The gurney sat beside the recliner.

"Can we take him, Lieutenant?"

"Ask Crime Scene. If they've got all their pictures and

whatever else they want, you can have him."

Miss Pavlov came in carrying a hand vacuum cleaner. "Looking for hair samples and the like," she said. "I already picked up a few strands of long blond hair." She nodded toward the dark-haired Mrs. Cooper-Svan in the living room. "Not hers, for sure."

Columbo nodded. "There's dust on the carpet, here and in the living room. Is that dust from the basement? Might suck up a sample and have it compared."

"I'm afraid it may have been tracked up by us."

"Maybe. Uh— Wait a minute here. Looka this." He got down on his hands and knees and peered at a whitish footprint. "Get a picture of this, Pavlov."

"Sir?"

"It's kinda vague, but I'd call this the footprint of a bare foot. Wouldn't you?"

Pavlov got down beside him and stared at the mark. "Yeah."

"Now, wouldn't that be interestin'? Lift a sample of that dust after you get your picture. Did somebody go down in the basement barefoot and come back up here carryin' dust on their feet? Curious, wouldn't you say?"

"I guess there's a whole lot of curious things about this case, Lieutenant."

Columbo nodded. "That's a fact. Some way, some parts of it don't make sense."

FRIDAY, JULY 31—NOON

Columbo did not sign out until nearly 3:00 A.M., and he did not check in at headquarters until 11:00. A man was entitled to some sleep, and he never felt right when he didn't get his eight hours. He drank coffee and ate a couple of the hard-boiled eggs Mrs. Columbo always left in the refrigerator in case he would not come down to breakfast at the usual time. He had a bit of difficulty getting his car started, which brought him to Parker Center a little later than he had intended.

Apart from the usual departmental memos and telephone notes saying he'd had many calls from news media people, nothing required his attention. He called Adrienne Boswell and asked if she would like to meet him for lunch at Burt's, for a game of pool and a bowl of chili. In this case, the murder of Gunnar Svan, Adrienne was a *witness*.

Adrienne had become—almost, not quite—a regular at Burt's. The real regulars did not know how to cope with the striking, tall woman with the flaming red hair and green eyes. She came in to play pool with Columbo—which was something else they did not understand, particularly since she beat him regularly. Today she was wearing skintight blue jeans and a white T-shirt, also spectacularly tight. She took a table and practiced shots while she waited for Columbo to arrive. The regulars were fascinated to see her practice bank shots.

"Hiya, Adrienne! Gonna beat me? Y' know, it's cheatin' to *practice.*"

"If I can endure the chili in here, you can endure losing dollar nine-ball, Columbo."

He laughed. "Hey! Ya look grand!"

"Thank you. So do you. A raincoat in July, when it hasn't rained for three weeks. Is that what every well-dressed man in Los Angeles wears?"

"Well now, Adrienne. You know how it is. I got so much stuff in my pockets."

"A hard-boiled egg?" she asked with a broad grin. "If so, is it *today's* hard-boiled egg?"

Columbo checked his pockets. "Actually I don't have an egg today. But I got somethin' else." He reached into his jacket pocket and withdrew a long yellow pencil. "See? Mrs. Columbo put a pencil in my pocket this morning, and I still got it. How's George?"

"Dan. Dan's just fine. He proposed marriage night before last. Again."

"Y' gotta marry that guy, Adrienne. Or marry some other guy, 'fore *I* get interested in ya. You're the only woman I ever met who could threaten my marriage."

Adrienne laughed. "If I thought you were serious, I'd hang up my cue and leave."

"Ahh . . . I got a daughter your age. Mrs. C and I were married before you were born. I just stand a step or two back and look, Adrienne. And think about when I was young. And I think about when the missus was."

"I bet Mrs. Columbo was beautiful."

"*She still is.* Hey! You've got to meet her. She's always been beautiful, whatever age. But you're right. When I married her, every guy I knew was green with envy. I was marryin' the best-lookin' girl in the neighborhood. They all wanted her, and I got her. She was Irish, and I was Italian, and the wisdom was that we could never get along together. But we did. I don't know if she's ever had second thoughts, but I never have."

"That's a lovely story, Columbo."

"Yeah . . . Right. Thank ya. I had to look at somethin' gruesome last night. I could use a bowl of Burt's chili right now, to settle my stomach."

"Right. You got the Gunnar Svan case."

"Different relationship between us on that, Adrienne. Official this time. You're a witness. I understand you were with Mrs. Cooper-Svan from— Well, from when to when?"

She nodded. "I know. Okay. She showed up at Umberto's about eight o'clock, a little after. She left at, like, ten, give or take a few minutes. I'm not the only witness. I mean, she's a well-known figure. Half a dozen people—or twice that—will testify they saw her there."

"Okay," said Columbo.

"To get to Umberto's by eight, she'd had to have left home by seven-thirty."

"Svan died between seven and nine, something like that. Being with you at the restaurant is not an alibi, exactly."

"Does she *need* an alibi?"

"When a spouse is murdered, it's always useful for the other spouse to have an alibi. Y' know? It's not essential, but it's always useful."

Adrienne chalked her cue. "Break?"

"Go ahead."

She slammed the cue ball into the rack, scattering balls and sinking the three. "Well, that's all I can say. She was at Umberto's from eight till ten."

"How was she doin', Adrienne? What kind of mood was she in?"

"If you're asking me if she was in the kind of mood a woman might be in who'd just beaten her husband to death, I can tell you she was calm, cordial, businesslike. We had business to talk, and we talked it."

"None of my business—"

"Oh, but I'll tell you. There were rumors about how the marriage was falling apart. She talked about Gunnar. She said he had his faults. She said he drank too much and that he had affairs. But she said he was an artist and that she could live with his idiosyncrasies." Adrienne paused and grinned. "She talked me into posing nude for *Glitz*."

"Adrienne!"

She grinned at him as she bent over the table and sank the one ball, then the two ball. "How 'bout that, Columbo? Will you buy a copy of the magazine?"

"I can't believe it. Or can I? Well . . . I mean . . . why not? You're a gorgeous woman, Adrienne."

"*Glitz* publishes very modest, tasteful nudes."

"Anyway—" said Columbo.

"If the woman had killed him half an hour before she came to the restaurant, goddamn I would have known something was wrong! How could she have sat there and calmly talked business when—?"

"She told you her husband had affairs? I mean, she out-right *said* that?"

"The whole damned town knows it. She could hardly have denied it."

"And she was putting up with it?"

"She's a poor little rich girl, Columbo. She could have

married— I bet she had a hundred proposals. So she finds this great, admired, artistic film director in Sweden: a cult figure. A *fraud* cult figure, in the mold of Jerzy Kosinski. She brings him to the States and uses her money to make him a cult figure here. Only it doesn't work too well. He's not the success here that he was in Sweden."

"Who'd he have affairs with?"

Adrienne missed a tough shot on the four, and Columbo moved up to shoot.

"I can name just one. There's an exotic dancer around town—a stripper—by the name of Pamela Starr, real name Murphy. The story is that he's had a torrid affair with her, so torrid that he bought her an expensive car. She's not the only one, though."

"Made his wife look foolish, I suppose," Columbo suggested.

Adrienne shook her head. "She sat down with me at eight o'clock. We had a couple of drinks, then dinner. We talked business. She gave me an interview, which included comments about her husband. If she had murdered him, in the way the news media say he was murdered, she would have been spattered with his blood within the last hour. No, Columbo. The woman I had dinner with had not been drenched in her husband's blood in the hour before."

1:21 P.M.

A police barrier of yellow plastic tape had been strung around the Cooper-Svan premises, and a black-and-white sat in the driveway. The death of the Swedish film director had not caused the media fury the death of Regina had caused the year before, but a few curiosity-seekers had come by, so the house remained guarded.

When Columbo pulled his car into the driveway, the officer got out.

"Columbo, Homicide."

"I recognize you, Lieutenant."

"Is Mrs. Cooper-Svan at home?"

"No. She left the house a while ago. Half an hour ago. The maid's in there."

Columbo rang the bell, and the maid came to the door. He introduced himself, and she said she was Mrs. Yasukawa. She wore the uniform of a maid: a rather drab gray dress and a white apron. She was a diminutive and exceptionally pretty young woman. She wore bright red lipstick.

"I'd like to ask you two or three questions, if you don't mind."

"Come in."

The door to the den was open. The recliner was gone, and the carpet had been taken up. Someone had worked there in the morning, beginning the process of cleaning.

Mrs. Yasukawa led Columbo into the kitchen, where he sat down at the table where he had last night sat with Lieutenant Lawrence and Martha Zimmer. He accepted a cup of coffee, and the maid poured one for herself.

"Mrs. Yasukawa, explain to me what's going on in the laundry room."

She did. She told him about how the washer scooted across the floor and how the bolted-down two-by-fours would keep it in place.

"What time did you leave here yesterday?"

"About five o'clock."

"Is that your usual time?"

"No. Usually I stay until about six-thirty. I leave after I have served dinner. When I come in the morning the dishes are in the dishwasher."

"And yesterday?"

"Mrs. Cooper-Svan told me I could leave at five. Mr. Svan would be late, so she asked me to make something that could be warmed up in the microwave and leave it so she could serve dinner when he came home. I left a lasagna in the microwave and a salad in the refrigerator."

"Okay. Well, thank ya, Mrs. Yasukawa. You've been very helpful." He sipped the last of his coffee. It was excellent. "I 'preciate it. I know the way out."

"Any cooperation, Lieutenant. I want to know who did this horrible thing."

"So do I, Mrs. Yasukawa. So do I. And, uh—" He stood at the kitchen door. "I guess I do have one more little question. You know how it is. In this business we have to tie up every loose end. Prob'ly isn't important, but the only way I know how to figure out cases is to get every possible fact in mind. Every trade has its trade secrets, and so far as I can figure out the trade secret of the detective trade is— Well . . . I'm ramblin' on. Anyway, I do have a question, if ya don't mind."

"Yes?"

"Mrs. Cooper-Svan went out to dinner, so I guess only one serving was eaten—"

"No. Two people ate dinner. I found dirty dishes for two people. *All* the salad was gone. All but a little of the lasagna. A bottle of wine. Two glasses. Two people ate dinner, Lieutenant Columbo."

"Very interestin'. Uh . . . you've *washed* those dishes."

She nodded. "The dishwasher."

4:30 P.M.

"Doc, I wouldn't have your job for a million bucks," Columbo said to Dr. Harold Culp.

"You've said that before, you know. A lot of people say it. I get tired of hearing it. The only time when it's nauseating is when you've got one that's decomposed. When we get one of those, I breathe from an air tank, wear clothes that won't absorb the stench, and the exhaust fans run like mad. Oh— Well— There are other times. Kids . . . Having to do an autopsy on a child does get to you, Columbo." The doctor shook his head. "That's tough, emotionally. I guess that's the hardest thing I have to do."

"Sorry I mentioned it."

They sat at the doctor's desk in his office outside the autopsy room. Columbo smoked a cigar. Dr. Culp was drinking Pepsi from a can. They had worked together on fifty cases, maybe a hundred, and knew each other as friends.

"So what do we know?" Columbo asked. "Can you come any closer on time of death?"

"Between seven and eight. Assuming he ate his dinner between six and seven."

"Okay."

"We find the guy slumped in a reclining chair, right?"

"Right."

" 'Slumped' is a good word, Columbo. Let's start off with this. The blood-alcohol percentage is point one-nine percent—almost twice what it takes to be considered drunk for driving purposes. In other words, Svan was schnocked out of his mind when he died. Now— Our scenario was that someone sneaked up behind him. Right?"

"Right."

"Wrong. He was struck from the front. Three times. The hardest blow—maybe the first one—broke through the frontal bone of the skull. The weapon itself crushed a considerable area of the frontal lobe of the brain. More than that, it drove bone fragments all the way into the corpus callosum."

"Which means?"

"It means it killed him. Crushed the brain— The blood loss—" The doctor shook his head. "Anyway, the brain took three such shocks, crushing much of it and driving bone fragments into the rest."

"How much strength would this take, Doc?"

"That depends on the weapon. If it was heavy— You're asking if a woman could have done it. The answer is yes, a woman could have done it."

"You know what a star drill is?" Columbo asked.

Dr. Culp nodded.

"Take one about as big as your thumb—"

"A boy or girl of ten could hit hard enough with one of those things."

Columbo puffed on his cigar and ran his left hand through his hair. "From in front. Somebody could have hit him from behind, right? But chose to hit from in front. Wonder why?"

Dr. Culp smiled. "That's why I prefer my job to yours. You have to answer questions like that, and I don't."

"Okay."

"Contents of stomach. A full meal—pasta, meat, cheese, tomato sauce—"

"Lasagna."

"Lasagna. Thank you. Salad. Wine. Gin. Cognac. Coffee."

"How much lasagna?" Columbo asked.

"Important?"

"Could be."

"I weighed the total contents of the digestive tract and didn't try to separate things out."

"Had he eaten a normal meal, is the point. Or had he gorged himself?"

"Normal meal," said Dr. Culp. "Except for the excessive alcohol, it was what you'd expect in the innards of a man who had dined well but had not gorged himself."

"So—"

"I'm not finished, Columbo. Within . . . let us say two or three hours of his death, Gunnar Svan engaged in— How do I say it? Hard sex. His vesiculae seminales were almost empty. He had ejaculated repeatedly. His penis was in an inflamed state. He'd done an athletic job—with somebody."

Columbo grinned and shook his head. "Now that makes for an awkward question. Am I supposed to ask Mrs. Cooper-Svan—? Oh, boy!"

Captain Sczciegel caught up with Columbo in the hall.

"Columbo, Columbo, Columbo! Damn it, man, I'm getting bitchy calls from the chief. Why've I got a detective on my staff who hasn't been to the range and qualified with his sidearm? You answer the question, Columbo? Why've I got that? How'm I s'pposed to explain it?"

Captain Sczciegel (who pronounced his name "Seagull") was a tall, thin, bald, harried man. He tried to steer a dif-

ficult middle course between strict adherence to proce-
dures, as prescribed in endless directives that were supposed to be filed in loose-leaf binders, and practical police
work. Columbo's sidearm wasn't the only burden the un-
kempt detective imposed on him; he was painfully aware
that Columbo did not even *have* ring binders and casually
tossed official directives in the trash.

(In fact, Columbo had told him once, "Way I figure, Captain, if something I *really* have to know comes along, you
or somebody else will tell me.")

"Actually, Cap'n," said Columbo, "I need some more time
to get myself acclimated to that gun. Y' see, I can't figure
out how to tell when it's loaded and when it's not. I hate
to carry around a gun, not knowing if there's a bullet right
under the hammer or not. And how can you tell if it's
cocked? If it is, an' it's loaded, that gun is *dangerous!* Now
that other gun I had—"

"Columbo—"

"The revolver, you know, was a whole lot easier to understand. I mean, I could see how it worked. This new gun
is just plain mysterious."

"But you didn't carry the revolver either."

"Well, I kept forgettin' it. Like, every morning Mrs.
Columbo puts a nice new yellow pencil in my pocket, and
a little notebook. But she was always afraid to touch the
gun, even the old gun. Now that we got orders to carry
those Italian guns—"

"Berettas, Columbo."

"Yeah. Us Italian guys make great lovers and great mu-
sicians, but—"

"The Beretta is one of the finest handguns ever made,
Columbo."

"Is that so? Well, I should have more respect for it, I
guess. It does worry me, though. I can't tell if it's—"

"Yeah, loaded. I know. Here's an order from the chief. Go out to the range and qualify with your sidearm, Lieutenant!"

"Right. Right, Cap'n. I'll do that . . . soon as I figure out who killed Mr. Svan."

"Who killed him, Columbo? I'm sure you've got it figured out."

"Well . . . Captain Sczciegel, I hate what I gotta tell ya. One hundred percent off the record, okay? I hate it. But— Mrs. Svan did it. I can't prove it. I may never be able to prove it. But I figure she did it. Off the record."

"Let's see you make your case, then. Let's see you prove it."

"That's the hard part, Cap'n. Isn't it always?"

SIX

SATURDAY, AUGUST 1

Ai-ling went to her office Saturday morning. She called Link and asked him to join her. While she waited for him she read her mail, then the newspapers, then went over layouts for two photo spreads that would appear in the October issue of *Glitz*. She dictated a memo to Bill Lloyd, telling him to save four pages for an article about Adrienne Boswell, accompanied by pictures. That was to have priority.

Link arrived before ten.

"Should you be here? Should you be working? Shouldn't you be at home grieving?" he asked, not without a hint of sarcasm in his voice.

"I needed to be away, to be with somebody. Top Gun is being cremated this morning." She glanced at her watch. "Probably right now. You *will* escort me to the funeral this afternoon?"

"Well, I'm not sure we should be seen together so often, Eileen."

"You're my *shrink,* for Christ's sake! Plus my friend. Who else—? And, incidentally, why don't you call me by my real name at long last? People who really know me do."

"Ai-ling. It will take a little getting used to. But any-way— That detective was looking at us with some suspicion Thursday night."

Ai-ling grinned. "That creep? Did you see him crawling around on the floor? We're smart people, you and I, Link. The day we can't outsmart some dumb LAPD bureau-crat—"

Link nodded. He sat down. He was wearing golfing clothes: tan slacks and a yellow knit shirt. Except for her call, he would have gone out to play golf.

Ai-ling lit a cigarette. She was wearing a black dress. She did not intend to go home and change before the fu-neral.

"I can't believe you did it," Link said solemnly. "I didn't think you would."

"Oh, I didn't. He was killed by an irate father," she said blandly.

"Sure. And the Buddha . . . ?"

"I smashed the case and removed it to confuse the mat-ter. A million-dollar burglary."

"What are we going to do with it?"

"I've been thinking. We might destroy it. In any case, I'll collect the insurance money."

"Ei— Ai-ling!"

She smiled lazily and shook her head. "There's nothing dishonest in that. I'm losing a million-dollar Buddha and recovering one million dollars. If I kept possession of the Buddha *and* collected the insurance, *that* would be dis-honest. What did I pay the premiums for, all those years? In case something happened to it, I'd get its value in money. Well . . . something's going to happen to it."

"You're a different woman, Ai-ling. I never knew you to be like this."

"People have taken me for a fool and played me for a fool," she said. "I got tired of it. I'm not Eileen Cooper-Svan. I'm Ai-ling Cooper. My great-grandmother, Peng Ai-ling, sailed the world with my great-grandfather. I'm named for her. She was as tough as he was. I have something for you," she said. She opened a door in her credenza and took out a ledger-sized checkbook. She wrote a check, payable to Dr. Lincoln Hilliard—one thousand dollars. "Here you are."

"What's this?"

"Fee for your services as my psychiatrist. Being my psychiatrist, you can keep my secrets and can't testify against me."

"I will keep your secrets and won't testify against you anyway," he said as he shoved the check across the desk toward her. "I have a very different motive, as you know."

"You take the check and deposit it," Ai-ling said firmly. "It makes things very clean and positive. When that detective, Columbo, comes snooping around—which he will—you will be able to tell him not to ask personal questions about your patient."

Link folded the check and put it in his billfold. "Really— What *are* we going to do with the Buddha? Having it in my place makes me nervous."

"Makes *you* nervous? Every day it exists it risks buying me a seat in the gas chamber. But let's don't be precipitate. It—"

"I checked my computer encyclopedia this morning," said Link. "Jade is brittle. We can pound it to bits and flush the bits down the toilet."

"Let's think about it a little. Maybe we can do something better with it. I've been playing with an idea."

The silver urn containing the ashes of Gunnar Svan sat on a small, draped table at the front of St. Michael's Lutheran Church. The pastor had been reluctant to conduct the funeral service on Sunday. Ai-ling had not wanted to wait until Monday. So the funeral was being held only a day and a half after the death. After the funeral, they would carry the urn to a mausoleum, where it would be sealed in a little vault.

Mrs. Columbo had pressed a black suit and had retied Columbo's necktie, to be sure the wide end hung below the narrow end. She had insisted he not wear his raincoat. Maybe she'd press that, too, while he was out. Better yet, maybe she'd burn it, so he'd have to buy a new one. Anyway, he didn't need it today. He was going to a funeral, not out to work. He had said going to the funeral was work, part of his job, but he had left the raincoat in the hall closet.

"Columbo!"

"Adrienne. How many funerals does this make where we've run into each other?"

"It's not coincidence. You're here doing your job. I'm here doing mine."

As they stood just outside the church, a silver BMW stopped at the curb half a block away. A garish-looking woman got out. Her hair was piled high. She wore a black dress, but it was skin-tight. She wore spike heels, and her bottom twitched as she walked into the church.

Columbo looked at Adrienne with a quizzical frown. "Uh . . . Friend of Mr. Svan, you suppose?"

"Pamela Murphy," said Adrienne. "Professionally, Pam Starr. Gunnar Svan made her a gift of the BMW. I don't expect Ai-ling Cooper-Svan is going to be happy to see *her* here."

They entered the church. It was by no means full. Gunnar's brother and sister had not flown to Los Angeles. A few reporters were present, as were twenty or thirty people from the film industry. Beverly Tree was there, with her husband. She sat in the front-left pew, as did Drake Rogers.

Pamela Murphy sat in the left rear corner of the church, at the end of the last pew.

Ai-ling arrived, on the arm of Link Hilliard, and they walked to the front. She glanced around at the people and nodded, with a faint smile, to the actors seated to her left.

The organist played "Nearer My God to Thee."

During the music a girl slipped quietly into the church and sat down in the rear. Adrienne nudged Columbo and whispered, "Ingrid Karlsen." He turned around to glance at the striking teenage girl. "I'll explain later," Adrienne whispered.

The minister spoke briefly about Gunnar Svan. He had been, he said, a faithful member of the church, a frequent attender, and a generous giver, who would be much missed. Then he asked the congregation to join him in prayer, and he read from the Bible the promises of eternal life.

Drake Rogers delivered the eulogy. He spoke of Gunnar Svan as an artist and a great film director whose films would be remembered and shown when most of what he called the fluff the industry turned out would be forgotten. He called Gunnar a kindly, supportive man who was ever ready to help his actors and his crews. "We have all learned a great deal about our craft from him, and that will be his legacy."

The minister prayed. After the prayer, Columbo turned around to have a better look at Ingrid Karlsen. She was gone. So was Pamela Murphy.

MONDAY, AUGUST 3—10:47 A.M.

Glitz published so much distinguished photography that it maintained a studio on the offices' premises. It had staff photographers, but its most important pictures were done by photographers hired on contract. Gilbert Gleason was one of the most honored photographers in the United States, and he was in the *Glitz* studios with his own cameras on Monday morning, ready to photograph Adrienne Boswell.

Adrienne had been astonished by Ai-ling's call on Sunday afternoon. She had agreed, of course, to be photographed for *Glitz,* but she had supposed that was something months away, for an issue sometime next year. She might change her mind, in time. When Ai-ling told her not only that she wanted to shoot on Monday morning for a photo spread in the next issue but that Gilbert Gleason would be the photographer, Adrienne didn't have time to think or find reasons to change her mind.

So here she was, on Monday morning, in a dressing room just off the studio, naked and being brushed with powder by a deferential technician. The technician with the brush was a woman. The artist doing the makeup was a man, as was the coiffeur.

Ai-ling had come in. She handed Adrienne a cup of coffee and a snifter of brandy. "Relax," she said. "Any woman with your face and body should be comfortable and proud."

"I never thought— And the man I love is thoroughly put off."

"When he sees the pictures, he'll be as proud as you and I are going to be."

Adrienne shook her head and smiled weakly. "God, I hope so. I do hope so. If you'd said anybody but Gil Gleason, I might have tried to back out. Well . . . To be photographed by him is like being painted by Renoir."

"That's exactly why I hired him, dear. You deserve the best."

Gleason was a small man with a carefully trimmed gray Vandyke beard and gold-rimmed round spectacles. By the time Adrienne entered the studio, he had arranged his setting and lighting. A neutral gray sheet had been rolled down from an overhead spool and pulled across the floor. Adrienne was to be photographed without props or a background, simply as a classic nude.

She was wearing a white wrapper, and he invited her to sit down and look through two albums. "My ballerinas," he said. "I love to photograph ballerinas. Such grace, as you can see. And perfect bodies . . . if perhaps a little too spare. Allow me to refill your glass."

By the time she walked out onto the neutral gray sheet, Adrienne's confidence in this venture had been augmented by the elegant ballerina nudes, and her tension had been all but eliminated by two more generous drinks of brandy.

Ai-ling remained in the studio throughout the two hours' shoot. When Gleason pronounced himself satisfied, she walked out onto the sheet where Adrienne had posed standing, seated, and lying, and said—

"I have an executive dining room. We can continue with *my* commitment to *you:* the interview."

The executive dining room could serve a dozen or so. One table was set aside in an alcove: a table for two. Ai-ling led Adrienne to that table.

"Gil and I agreed that posing you with drapery, even a negligee, would have been— How shall I put it? Coy. Anyway, doing it as we did, we got classic and beautiful pictures. His assistant did some Polaroids. I didn't bring those now. I want you to see the finished prints that Gil will come up with."

"I really felt quite comfortable, after a while."

"*I've* done it," said Ai-ling. "*I* was comfortable. I haven't published any of mine. Maybe I should. I'm not as perfect as you are."

The executive dining room was serving a poached salmon that day, with a chilled white chablis. Ai-ling ordered a margarita first, and Adrienne took a Scotch and soda.

"I saw you at the church yesterday. With Lieutenant Columbo. You and he are friends?"

"Yes. He's an odd character, but he's totally, one-hundred-percent shrewd. He'll figure out who killed Mr. Svan."

"Well, I hope so, for god's sake. And who stole the million-dollar jade Buddha." Ai-ling paused and drew a deep breath. "I'm going to tell you something, Adrienne. I'm not sure that the theft of the Buddha had anything to do with the murder of Gunnar. I have to think it may have been a diversion. Can you understand what I'm suggesting?"

"Not exactly."

"There are people with reasons for wanting Gunnar dead," said Ai-ling. "I'm going to let you listen to a snip-

pet of audiotape in a minute. Adrienne, no woman between sixteen and sixty was safe in his presence. I called
him Top Gun, and there was damned good reason for calling him that."

"I've heard that nickname," said Adrienne with a small
smile.

"Two of them came to the church yesterday afternoon,"
said Ai-ling. "The whore in the back corner . . . Pamela
Murphy. Gunnar gave her a $60,000 car—bought with my
money. The child in the rear middle pew. Ingrid Karlsen.
She's seventeen, and Gunnar seduced her with the
promise that he would make her a film star."

"I've heard there were others, to be perfectly frank,"
said Adrienne.

"One who's a hooker," said Ai-ling. "I shut him out of my
bed for fear of the microbiology he might have picked up."

"Audiotape?"

"Ingrid's father, Piers Karlsen, came to see me a couple
of weeks ago. I knew when his name was sent in what he
wanted. So—I have a taping system in my office. I taped
what he said. I have the tape here, with a little player and
an earplug. Want to hear it?"

Adrienne accepted the little player and put the plug in
her ear.

> "I'm saying your husband is corrupting my
> daughter."
>
> " 'Corrupting'? Please?"
>
> "Mrs. Svan— I told you. To put the matter in
> the bluntest words, your forty-year-old husband
> is fucking my seventeen-year-old daughter!"
>
> "Why don't you call the police?"
>
> "You don't believe me."
>
> "No, I don't. Gunnar is no angel, but I don't

think he is capable of seducing a seventeen-year-old girl. No . . . I don't think he's capable of that."

". . . she is living with your husband in his trailer, on a motion-picture set in Arizona. She says he has promised to make her the star of a picture he means to make, starting later this year. It is her dream. It is what she always wanted. Tell me, Mrs. Svan, will your husband really make my daughter a star?"

"If he does, is all forgiven?"

"I want her to be what she wants."

"We're not talking about virginity then, are we? We're not talking about corruption or seduction. We're talking about the girl getting what she's paying for. What is it you're asking me to do— rein in a straying husband or make him keep his promises to Ingrid?"

"Either one, Mrs. Svan."

"Suppose I can't?"

"In that case, I might have to deal with the matter some other way."

The tape went silent, and Adrienne pulled the plug from her ear. "Have you given this to Columbo?" she asked.

"Not yet. I wasn't sure what to do."

"Ai-ling, you've got to let Columbo hear this tape."

"I gotta tell you something more," said Ai-ling. She paused and sighed. "I go to New York all the time. I go to Europe. When I was away . . . Well— Gunnar brought his women home. I found evidence of it. Never mind what. Okay. Who knew about the Buddha? Who knows what creeps a woman like Pamela Murphy sees—who she told about a million-dollar jade statuette sitting in the living room? And there was a hooker. What kind of guys does *she* associate with? Simple. Easy. Come to the house—Murphy or the hooker—and get let in. Together with a boyfriend who smashes Gunnar's brains in and leaves with a million dollars' worth of jade."

"Do you want to take the tape to Columbo? Or do you want me to?"

"I'd be glad if you'd do it, Adrienne. Frankly, I'm weary of talking about Gunnar, of thinking about him. He was far from perfect. He wasn't the man I thought I'd married. But—" She shook her head. "—to have to think of him . . ."

"I'll give Columbo the tape."

4

4:13 P.M.

Adrienne sat at Columbo's desk at police headquarters and watched his reaction as he listened to Ai-ling's tape. From a paper cup she sipped some of the worst coffee she had ever tasted in her life.

As Columbo pulled the earplug out and handed the player back to Adrienne, Captain Sczciegel stopped at the desk.

"Are you going to introduce me, Columbo?"

"Yeah. Adrienne Boswell. Adrienne, this is Captain Sczciegel. He's my boss."

"I'm pleased to meet you, Miss Boswell. I've read some of your stuff. I guess Columbo has given you a few tips from time to time."

Adrienne looked up at the tall captain, bald as a cue ball. He was without a jacket, and his shirtsleeves were rolled back to his elbows. She smiled and trusted he didn't realize that what she was smiling at was the heavy automatic pistol that hung awkwardly in his armpit. "Turnabout," she said. "Today I've brought Columbo a tip."

"Y' oughta listen to it, Cap'n. Pull up a chair and listen to an interestin' tape. Conversation between Mrs. Cooper-Svan and a fella named Piers Karlsen."

Captain Sczciegel pulled a chair away from another detective's desk, sat down, put the plug in his ear, and listened gravely to the dialogue. When it was finished he bestowed a knowing little smile on Columbo and said, "Maybe you jumped to a conclusion a little too fast."

Columbo nodded. "That's possible, isn't it? Maybe I did. We'll see."

"That's helpful, Miss Boswell. I know you have a right to keep your sources confidential, but can we know where you got this tape?"

"No problem. Eileen Cooper-Svan gave it to me."

"Adrienne's gonna be featured in the September issue of *Glitz*," said Columbo. "She posed for some nude pictures this morning."

Captain Sczciegel's eyebrows rose, and he grinned. "I'll buy *that* issue," he said.

"I'll autograph it for you."

"So, Columbo," the captain said, self-conscious and turning businesslike, "we seem to have a plethora of scenarios. I'd supposed the theft of a million-dollar jade statuette was motive enough for the murder. But now— Now you've got an outraged father, too."

"Why would he steal the Buddha?" Columbo asked.

"I can think of two reasons," said Adrienne. "First, why would he *not* steal a million dollars' worth of jade art? Second, he could have stolen the Buddha to cover his real motive for killing Svan."

"I don't much like your first motive," said Columbo. "You told me Piers Karlsen is the owner of a camera shop—"

"Photofinishing."

"Whatever. To fence that Buddha, a person would have to be very, very knowledgeable. *Whoever* stole it isn't gonna get a million dollars for it, or anywhere near. That property is *hot*. Theft, even burglary, is one thing, and murder is somethin' else again. A fence won't risk havin' that in his hands—unless it's a very specialized fence, probably with a buyer lined up beforehand."

"I like the way his mind works," said Captain Sczciegel. "It's why we tolerate him, Miss Boswell."

"She gave Adrienne two more names," Columbo said. "One's a stripper. Mrs. Cooper-Svan thinks Svan had the stripper in his house. If so, she undoubtedly saw the Buddha. Now. That kind of woman gets around. She hangs out places where all kinds of rotten characters come. And then there's a hooker. She could have some interestin' friends."

The captain smiled. "Looks like you've got some days' work cut out for you, Columbo."

SEVEN

Karlsen's photofinishing shop smelled of the chemicals that were sloshing around in the back room. Unconsciously, Columbo grimaced. The smell was sharp. It made his saliva flow, too.

He showed his badge to the man who came out and stood behind the counter. "Lieutenant Columbo, LAPD Homicide."

"Piers Karlsen," the man said with a faint trace of Swedish accent. It was the voice and accent Columbo had heard on the tape. Karlsen was a big fellow, muscular. Columbo wondered if he didn't have a double-bitted ax and a big blue ox somewhere. "I know who you are, Lieutenant. I see on the news that you are investigating the death of Gunnar Svan."

"That's a fact," said Columbo. "Uh . . . Gotta match? Hope you don't mind if I smoke a cigar. The smell of your chemicals kinda gets to me."

"You get used to them," said Karlsen. He reached under

the counter and handed over a book of paper matches imprinted with the name of his shop.

"Mr. Karlsen, you . . . uh, had a problem with Mr. Svan, didn't you?"

"He seduced my seventeen-year-old daughter."

Columbo nodded and ran his hand through his hair. "Right. She came to his funeral."

Karlsen's chin shot up. "No!"

"I'm afraid so, Sir. I saw her there. Well . . . I saw a girl who was identified to me as Miss Karlsen."

"I told her not to go. I *begged* her not to go. I have no control over her anymore."

"She's a very pretty girl," said Columbo.

Karlsen nodded. "Sometimes I've wished she wasn't. It's been the source of a lot of the difficulty I've had with her."

Columbo puffed on his cigar and carefully blew his smoke toward the floor on his side of the counter. "Mr. Karlsen, it would be to your great advantage if you could tell me where you were between, say, seven and nine on the evening of Thursday, July thirtieth."

"I can tell you where I was, alright. But I can't prove it."

"Maybe I can. You tell me where you were."

"I close the shop about six. Usually I don't get away much before six-thirty, because I have to take care of the last pictures developing and being fixed and drying. Sometimes I stay considerably later, to do a special order. That night, I think I got away from here about six-thirty, six-forty-five at the latest. I got home. Ingrid wasn't there. She was supposed to be but she wasn't."

"Was she supposed to fix your dinner?"

"Frankly, yes. *Our* dinner. She wasn't there, and I don't know where she was."

"Okay."

"I put a microwave pizza in the oven, opened a beer, and

sat down to dinner. And the phone rang. I figured it would be Ingrid with some dishonest explanation of where she was and what she was doing. But it wasn't. It was a woman. She said her name was Brenda. She'd called me earlier that afternoon, at the shop, and suggested we get together for a drink. She said she was a customer and that I'd know her when I saw her. I said okay. I couldn't place her, but I said okay. What th' hell?"

"She calls you, sort of out of a clear blue sky, and asks you to—"

"Lieutenant— I'm not a bad-lookin' guy. I'm single, a widower. I get . . . invitations."

" 'Kay. So?"

"She said I should meet her at the corner of Wilshire and Western. She said she'd be driving a white Pontiac and that I should give her half an hour."

"And?"

"Well, I got there, like, about a quarter till eight. And I waited for her for the better part of an hour. She didn't show up, so I went home."

Columbo ran his hand over his head, ruffling his hair. "So, like you said, you got no witnesses to verify your story."

Karlsen raised his hand and indicated that a customer was coming in. Columbo looked around the shop, at a display of prints and frames, while Karlsen received a roll of film for processing.

"Okay." Karlsen sighed noisily when the customer was out the door. "Am I a suspect in the murder of Gunnar Svan?"

"I don't know for sure, Mr. Karlsen. Maybe you oughtn't talk to me."

"I've got nothing to hide."

"I hope not. But on Saturday of the week before the murder you went to the office of Mrs. Cooper-Svan and accused Mr. Svan of seducing your daughter. Do you remember the conversation?"

"Yes."

"Well, Mrs. Cooper-Svan maintains a taping system in her office and taped what you said. I've listened to that tape."

"I didn't threaten."

"Uhmmm . . . Depends on how you read it. You said what you really wanted from Mr. Svan was the movie role he had promised your daughter. You also said that if Mrs. Cooper-Svan couldn't arrange that, you might have to find other ways to deal with the matter. You want to deny that's what you said?"

"Not at all. But what other ways I was talking about didn't include killing the man. I was thinking about a lawsuit, or about bringing in the police."

"Did you ever talk to Mr. Svan himself?"

"No. I'll be frank with you, Lieutenant. I might have been tempted to bash his nose in. *A seventeen-year-old girl,* Lieutenant!"

"When did she last see him, Mr. Karlsen?"

"I don't know."

"Was she still seeing him after he came home from Arizona?"

"I don't know. I suppose so."

"She hoped to get into the movies. You hoped she would."

"Lieutenant, she'd been sleeping with the man for a month! She couldn't get her virginity back. She hadn't had any to give him. But out of what she gave him, she was entitled to *something!* If he could make her *happy,* Lieutenant! If he could give her what would make her happy—"

"I have to talk to her."

"Call me this evening. Maybe she'll be home."

"Oh, well, I'm sorry. I should have called for an appointment."

"I'm sorry, but you should've, Lieutenant. I'm sure Dr. Hilliard wants to give you every cooperation, but he does have a patient with him and a patient waiting. After that—" She flipped the pages of her book, then shook her head. "Dr. Hilliard has a full schedule of appointments today. I suppose, for a homicide detective, we could squeeze you in between—"

"No, no. That's okay. I'll call and set up an appointment."

"We mean to help, I'm sure."

"Well, I don't want to talk about a patient, where the doctor has an obligation to keep a confidence. I only want to ask a question or two about a friend."

"About—?"

"About Mrs. Cooper-Svan."

The woman frowned. "But Mrs. Cooper-Svan *is* a patient."

"Oh . . . Well, I didn't know that. So maybe I can't ask the doctor anything."

"I am sure Dr. Hilliard will extend every possible cooperation."

"Of course, of course. No doubt. So—"

"Would half an hour sometime tomorrow be convenient, Lieutenant?"

"Let's let it go for now. I'll phone."

The woman smiled cordially. "Certainly. We can almost

always squeeze someone in, given a day's notice."

"I thank ya. I do. Very nice of you." He turned and started for the door, then paused. "Oh. Oh, there is one little thing. Little question. Uh— How long has Mrs. Cooper-Svan been a patient of Dr. Hilliard's?"

"She's been a personal friend for a long time, Lieutenant. A patient more recently."

"Maybe because difficult problems came up?"

"Lieutenant . . . I wouldn't know, and if I did I couldn't say."

1:09 P.M.

"Hiya, Marge," Columbo said to the woman behind the counter. "Gotta see a jacket. One Muriel Paul."

" 'Kay, Lieutenant," the woman said. She was a records clerk. "Need to check it out?"

"No. Just look."

While he waited, he fished the stub of a cigar out of his raincoat pocket, looked at it for a moment, then decided to return it to his pocket.

Marge returned with the file. He glanced through it. What he figured. There was more in it than Mrs. Cooper-Svan knew. Muriel Paul had been arrested a dozen times, usually for prostitution but once for grand theft, auto, and once for breaking and entering. The serious charges had been dropped in return for her cooperation. The notes of the detective who had arrested her for breaking and entering said she was probably an unwitting accomplice, at least at first. She was none too bright, the detective said. Her boyfriend had broken into the liquor store and then opened the door and let her in. While they were gathering up cases of liquor to carry out to his car, two black-and-whites arrived in response to the store alarm system that had alerted the police. The boyfriend, who had a long record, was serving his time. The auto theft seemed to have happened the same way. A group of men were stealing them, and Muriel Paul just went along. Her mug shots showed a big, unhappy girl.

"Hey, Marge. Ya got a jacket for Pamela Murphy?"

She did. She came out with that one after a minute or two. Pamela Murphy had been arrested for shoplifting ten years ago. She was placed on probation for two years, after which she was given an unconditional release. Her mug shot was barely recognizable as the woman he had seen at the Svan funeral.

"Got anything on a guy named Piers Karlsen?"

Marge looked and came back saying Karlsen had no arrest record with LAPD.

"Well, thank ya, Marge. Always a pleasure to do business with you."

4

2:11 P.M.

Columbo took a seat on a stool at the counter of the shop called JUST DONUTS. It was doing slow business at this time of day. The counter girls were dressed in tight red T-shirts and skimpy white shorts. One of them came over and asked what he'd like.

He showed her his badge. "Columbo, LAPD Homicide. I'm lookin' for Muriel Paul."

"That's me."

"I'm lucky you're not workin' the midnight shift this week," he said.

"It's not lucky for me. We don't do nearly the business during the day that we do at night."

"Which cuts your tips."

"Which cuts my tips. I saw in the paper where you're lookin' into the murder of Gunnar."

Muriel Paul was a big young woman. *Horsy* was the word that came to Columbo's mind. Her hair, obviously but inexpertly bleached, was dishwater blond. Her features were oversized and coarse, and her cheeks were pitted with a few acne scars. Even so, she was pretty— vulnerable-looking and appealing.

"Tell me about Gunnar."

Muriel shrugged. "I saw him a few times. You know why."

"Right. If I can believe your rap sheet, you've gone outa that line of work. Haven't been arrested in two years."

"I only do it occasionally, when some really nice guy offers really good money."

"And Gunnar did?"

She nodded. "I'm sorry to lose the guy. He was good for a hundred every so often."

"When was the last time you saw him?"

"About a month before he . . . died. He called me and asked me to come out in the desert where he was shooting a picture. I drove over to Arizona. He gave me two hundred for that time."

"Did he ever take you to his house?"

"A coupla times, when his wife was outa town. He'd call and say he was lonesome."

"Did you ever see the jade Buddha?"

"Oh, yeah. He was really proud of that thing. I don't know why. It belonged to his wife."

"Did he tell you how much it was worth?"

"Yeah."

The manager of the doughnut shop came out of the kitchen. "You gonna sell the man a doughnut and coffee, Muriel? Or is this your social hour?"

"Butt out, Randy. This is Lieutenant Columbo. He's a homicide detective. I'm bein' interrogated."

"Ohh. Who'd she murder, Lieutenant?"

"Three cops and a cab driver," said Columbo.

Randy went back to the kitchen.

"So, what can I do for you?" Muriel asked.

"Oh, nothin' much. I'm just talkin' to all his friends."

"So how'd you find out about me?"

"Mrs. Cooper-Svan knew about you."

"Huh-uh. She may have known who I was, but she didn't know what my name was or where to find me."

"She knew your name."

"How?"

Columbo ran his hand through his hair. He tipped his head to one side and shrugged. "That's a good question," he said.

2:45 P.M.

He flagged down a black-and-white, showed his badge, and asked to use the radio.

"Hiya," he said to the dispatcher. "This is Lieutenant Columbo, Homicide. I need to get in touch with Sergeant Zimmer. I couldn't get her on the phone, so I guess she's out in her car somewhere."

The dispatcher radioed Zimmer and patched the call to the black-and-white.

"Hey, Martha. You got time to meet me at Burt's for a few minutes? I'll treat ya to a root beer."

"Be there in about twenty minutes, Columbo."

When Martha arrived at Burt's, Columbo was sitting on a stool watching two men playing eight ball.

"What can I do for you, Columbo?"

"There's a gal that works at a place called JUST DONUTS, on Melrose. Big blond. Y' can't miss her," said Columbo. "She'll be gettin' off work at four o'clock. I'd like ya to put a tail on her. Not necessarily you, but somebody. What I wanta know is, has she got a regular boyfriend? If she does, who is he?"

"You wanta tell me what it's all about?"

"Well, there might just be a little coincidence waitin' for us. Probably not, but it's worth finding out. I mean, would she by any chance be seeing a guy who's a burglar or a fence?"

"You got it."

"Oh. One other little thing," Columbo said. "The contractor that was drillin' holes in the basement floor in the house on Loma Vista is named Craig. How 'bout stoppin' by and asking him if he'd wiped the dust off the drill for any reason."

6

7:21 P.M.

Ingrid Karlsen refused to talk with Columbo in the presence of her father. Piers agreed to leave the apartment and go out for a beer and pizza while the homicide detective questioned his daughter.

"You were at the funeral," she said.

"You've got a memory for faces."

The girl grinned. "You aren't the kind of guy somebody is likely to forget. For god's sake, take off the raincoat inside, would you? Want a beer?"

"I'm on duty."

"Bull. Rather have Scotch?"

"I'll take a beer."

"So will I. Now, don't tell me I'm underage."

"I'm homicide, not juvenile."

"Really think I'm a juvenile, Lieutenant?" she asked, preening herself. In a tiny blue mini-dress, she looked anything but juvenile. "I hardly ever see a man that thinks I'm not ripe."

She went to the kitchen for the beers, and he glanced around the apartment. It was modest, dominated by a twenty-six-inch television set on which some kind of early-evening comedy show was appearing. He turned down the volume.

He heard Ingrid pop open the beer cans, and she returned, handing him one.

"So— Poor Gunnar."

"He seems to have lived an interesting life."

The girl chuckled. "You can only guess. He was one hell of a guy, Lieutenant Columbo." She frowned and sighed. "He was going to make me a *star!*"

"I hear you lived with him a couple of weeks."

"*Glorious* couple of weeks. Then my old man showed up and bullied us."

"Bullied you?"

"Oh, big *daddy,* he made all kinds of noises. Gunnar told

me to come on home with him, that we'd fix things up later."

" 'Fix things up'? Like how?"

"Gunnar was going to divorce his old woman and marry me!"

Columbo smiled and drank from his can of beer.

"You don't think so," she said irritably. "Well, I'm gonna tell you, we had *plans!*"

"You ever go to his house? You ever see the inside of his house?"

"Well . . . Yeah. But that was his old woman's house. Gunnar and me, we were gonna live on a boat!"

"Exactly how old are you, Miss Karlsen?"

" 'Miss Karlsen,' if that's what you have to call me, will be eighteen next week. I told Gunnar I was already eighteen so— Well, you know why."

"Where were you the night he was killed?"

"Sitting right here, staring at that TV set."

"Where was your father?"

"I don't know. He wasn't here when I got home."

"Which was what time?"

"Quarter to eight. He'd microwaved a pizza and left a mess."

"What time did he get back?"

"Hey! Are you askin' these questions because you got some kind of idea my old man murdered Gunnar? 'Cause if you are, forget it. He's not man enough to step on an ant."

"What time did he get back?"

"I don't know," she said peevishly. "Nine. Nine-thirty."

"Well . . . Thanks for the beer." He took another swallow. "I gotta get home. Even a guy in my business has a wife and a home, and Mrs. Columbo's waitin' dinner." He stood and started toward the door.

"Columbo— Did you see Gunnar's body?"

He nodded.

"Are you sure it was him?"

"Several people identified him. Why?"

"Ohh . . ." She sighed. "I had an idea maybe he faked his death so he and I— I know it's not true, but—"

Columbo stared at her sympathetically. "No," he said quietly. "It's not true. Gunnar Svan is dead."

Ingrid nodded. "I'll tell you who killed him. His old woman. She found out he was going to leave her."

Columbo opened the door. "Uh . . . Y' know, I guess I oughta ask you one more thing. I mean, it's . . . uh, you know. Just one of those little facts that fills in a blank in the story. Uh, when did you see him last, Miss Karlsen?"

She shook her head. "You should have asked me that before."

"So?"

"It was . . . probably . . . two hours before he—" The girl sobbed. "He made love to me, Lieutenant Columbo! He made love to me like he'd never made love to me before! I mean, maybe he was afraid something was gonna happen to him, and maybe he wanted to—"

"Where, Miss Karlsen?"

"Up in the hills. In his car. We— I'm grateful I've got that memory of him, our last time together. I mean, Gunnar was a *stallion,* Lieutenant Columbo! There was nothing we didn't do for each other!"

"Well, uh— I see. I guess there's one more thing, Miss Karlsen. There was some blond hair found on the floor near Mr. Svan. Just a few strands. Now, uh . . . that couldn't have been yours, right? You weren't there."

"I wasn't there. That day. I'd been in the house before— two times when his wife was out of town."

"Would you mind giving me a few strands of your hair,

so our lab can compare? It would be helpful to know if that blond hair is yours or somebody else's."

Ingrid Karlsen gave a jerk on her hair and pulled out half a dozen long strands. "Need an envelope, Lieutenant?" she asked.

9:02 P.M.

"Hey, Pavlov. You'll get this message in the morning. This is Lieutenant Columbo. Listen, I've ordered guys to impound Gunnar Svan's car. 'Kay? I'd like you guys from Crime Scene to go over it. This is what you'll be lookin' for—"

EIGHT

WEDNESDAY, AUGUST 5—NOON

Ai-ling sat at a poolside table at the Pacifica Club.
She sipped from a margarita. Her eyes were covered with
dark sunglasses. She wore an iridescent blue bikini. She
had been swimming in the pool, and her hair was wet.

"Thank you very much," she said quietly to each of several people who stopped at her table to offer sympathy on
the loss of her husband. "It's kind of you."

Actually, of course, she didn't want to hear it. She wondered how long it would be before people stopped saying
it. Even if Gunnar had died of a heart attack, there would
have come a time when she wouldn't want painful re-
minders.

"May I join you for a moment?"

She looked up into the knife-sharp face of George Talbot. "Sit down, George," she said.

He was carrying a glass: gin and tonic, with a slice of
lime. He sat down and put his drink on the table.

"I understand you've made a coup. The story around is

---

that you're going to publish nudes of Adrienne Boswell."

"Well, you know how I publish nudes, George. Nothing sensational."

"It's a coup, just the same. And I congratulate you."

George was an agent and promoter. He had not approached her without a purpose. She wondered which one of his clients needed a boost.

"Would you be willing to do something to help out Jay Emerson?" he asked. Bluntly. Directly. "Doldrums. I suppose you've noticed."

"Doldrums? The problem with Emerson is, he hasn't got talent one. He's two-dimensional."

"He'll pose for—"

"*George.* It'd be cliché! Young actors with tight, hairless buns. He'd just be another one in the parade."

"When you ran Gig, his sagging career took off again."

"That was because Gig Boyer was a goody two-shoes. To see *him* in the altogether was a sensation. To see Jay Emerson would be a yawn. I have no doubt you can get somebody to run a spread on him—a whole lot more graphic than I'd run—but I can't see doing it in *Glitz.*"

Talbot smiled woodenly. "You can't blame me for trying."

"I *don't* blame you for trying. Keep me in mind."

"Like a little piece of gossip?" he asked. "Would you believe that Billie Cross spent a weekend in a Tahoe motel with Len Brewster?"

Ai-ling chuckled. "No, I wouldn't believe it." Billie Cross was a café singer who had come to Los Angeles from Detroit, where she had been only modestly successful, and here became a quick fad. Len Brewster was a Los Angeles city council member, reportedly interested in running for mayor. "Can you prove it?"

"No, I can't. But *you* can, if you want to. You have the resources to look into a story like that."

"Right. So, thanks, George. Sorry I can't do anything for your client, but there'll be others."

Link Hilliard arrived. He smiled at George Talbot and sat down.

"Let me introduce George Talbot. He's one of the most successful agents in town. George, this is Dr. Hilliard. He's my shrink. I've been leaning on his arm a lot the past few days."

"I neglected to express my sympathy. It's nice to meet you, Doctor Hilliard. I'll, uh, be moving on. Do check the tip, Eileen. If the story is true, it's got all the elements."

"It does, for sure."

Link watched Talbot working his way among the poolside tables, speaking to some people, nodding at others.

"Are we seeing each other too publicly?"

"You're my *doctor!*"

"Yeah. But I wasn't seeing you like this before."

"I didn't need a psychiatrist the way I do now. I've gone through a brutal trauma."

Link had left his jacket in the car but was still wearing a white shirt with a rep striped tie in dark green and dark red.

"I've had a brainstorm," said Ai-ling. "That's why I called you and asked you to meet me here. It won't wait for tonight."

"Beware of women suffering brainstorms."

"It's not a scientific term, is it? But listen— I've thought about what to do with the Buddha. A perfect idea."

"Beware of perfect ideas."

"Damnit, don't be negative about what you haven't heard. And don't be negative before you've heard it all. What I'm going to do with the Buddha is dump it on Piers Karlsen. Then I'll tip the cops as to where to find it."

Link stared silently at the reflections in her sunglasses,

unable to read her face without being able to see her eyes. "Well—?"

Link frowned deeply. "Why so anxious to hang Piers Karlsen? As of right now, Gunnar was killed by 'person or persons unknown.' You're in no danger. They haven't focused on you. It may be that Lieutenant Columbo will never solve the case. He doesn't impress me as being too bright."

"Adrienne tells me a sharp, shrewd mind hides behind that bumbling facade."

"I'd say reserve the idea until we need it."

"I'm grateful to hear you say it that way. 'We' need it."

"I love you, Ai-ling. You know that."

2:10 P.M.

Columbo sat down facing Ai-ling across her glass desk. The woman surprised him by her posture. She had to know that, sitting with her legs apart the way they were, he could see her legs through the glass, almost to the edge of whatever she was wearing for undies. But that was her posture: elbows on desk, legs apart.

"I'm sorry to bother you, Mrs. Cooper-Svan. I told you I'd have to ask one or two questions sooner or later."

"I expected to see you again long before now, Lieutenant."

"Well— I see you smoke. Would you mind if I light up a cigar?"

"Not at all."

He reached into his raincoat pocket, found a half-burned

butt, then decided he wouldn't let this lady see him re-lighting a chewed cigar. He took out a fresh one, tore off the cellophane, and ran it under his nose. He bit off the tip and carefully deposited that little piece in the pocket with the butt.

"I do sort of favor 'em. I never got so I could enjoy cigarettes. But a cigar— Well, that's somethin' else again. There's somethin' warm about smokin' a cigar. It sort of makes a man feel like he's his own friend."

"I never heard it put that way before. You're an interesting man, Lieutenant Columbo. Adrienne talked to me about you, a little. She says you've got quite a record of success. Maybe when you're all finished investigating the death of Gunnar we can run an article on you."

Columbo grinned. "Uh— Can I use your lighter? Me, I'd bore your readers. I'm just a sort of straightforward working guy. There's nothin' glamorous in what I do. I just run around, looking into things and asking questions, trying to make sense out of facts that usually don't fit together and sometimes contradict each other." He puffed and got his cigar lighted. "Who was it said getting anything done is one percent inspiration and ninety-nine percent perspiration?"

"Edison said that. 'Genius is one percent inspiration and ninety-nine percent perspiration.' "

"That's me. I go around makin' a nuisance of myself, pickin' up a fact here and a fact there."

"Well— Are there any facts you need from me?"

"A couple little things I wonder about. Probably don't amount to much."

"Let's hear them, Lieutenant."

"Well, Ma'am, I noticed that some dust had been tracked up from the cellar. I'm afraid some of that came up on the shoes of police personnel. But one footprint didn't, for sure.

One of the footprints—I'm almost sure of this—was from a bare foot. Can you give me any idea why a—"

"I can explain that," she interrupted. "Gunnar had a longtime habit, as long as I knew him, of running around the house barefoot. The evening he died he went down to the cellar to pick up a bottle of wine: Chianti with our lasagna. It was dusty down there. You know why."

"But the footprint I'm talking about was in the living room, just at the door of the den."

"He went down and got the bottle of wine, came up into the kitchen, and went to the den to turn off the television set before we sat down to dinner—as I'd asked him to do."

"I appreciate that, Ma'am. I can quit wonderin' about that."

"Anything else?"

"Well, there is one thing. Y' know the glass in the back door was broken. The shards of glass were lying on the kitchen floor. But one shard was in the grass outside. When glass is broken, the pieces fall away from the impact that broke it, not toward it. Could there have been somebody else in the house? I mean, like, hiding?"

Ai-ling turned down the corners of her mouth and shook her head. "Lieutenant, I haven't the remotest idea. When I left the house, he was passed-out drunk. If he had one of his girlfriends hidden away somewhere, maybe down in the cellar, I didn't know about it."

" 'Kay. Well, I guess I won't need to bother you anymore right now. I hope you won't mind if I come up with another question now and then."

"No, of course not. Anything I can do to help you identify the killer—"

"I 'preciate it. So I'll thank ya again for your time and be on my way."

"Anytime, Lieutenant Columbo. Anytime. And don't reject too quickly the idea of being featured in *Glitz*."

He stood and walked to the door. He could not resist looking one more time at her handsome legs through the glass top of the desk—though he had struggled to avert his eyes from them while they talked. He glanced at his cigar and decided he would not stub this one out and drop it in his pocket with the butt. He couldn't keep it alight in the elevator, so he decided to walk down.

"Lieutenant—"

"Ma'am?"

"You're frowning."

"Uh— Well. A little question did come to mind just now. Come to think of it. One more little thing and I'll be on my way. Just another one of those dumb little questions that prey on a man's mind and prob'ly don't mean a thing."

"What is it, Lieutenant?"

"Well, y' see, you gave Adrienne the names of some women who'd been, uh, intimate with Mr. Svan. Now, you said it wasn't the world's biggest deal with you; you forgave him. Two of them showed up at the funeral—Pamela Murphy, a stripper who works under the name Starr, which you might know about because in a town like this word of that kind of stuff gets around. Ingrid Karlsen, who you'd know because her father came and complained to you about it. Okay so far. But then you named Muriel Paul, a gal who works in skimpy shorts in a doughnut shop and has a record of arrests for prostitution. Where'd you get that name, Mrs. Cooper-Svan?"

Ai-ling blanched. "I don't know. Offhand, I— My husband left notes around. I . . ."

"No, Mrs. Cooper-Svan. Your husband's notes would not have said that Muriel had a police record, specifying for what. Maybe he didn't even know. You know an awful lot about Muriel Paul."

"This is getting into hostile interrogation, Lieutenant. I'm not sure I ought to talk to you without a lawyer present."

Columbo smiled and nodded. "You just used the magic word. No more talk until—"

"Now, hang on. I knew who Muriel Paul was because—Okay, Columbo. Gunnar was playing outside the rules. An affair here and there is one thing. He spent sixty thousand dollars of my money to buy the stripper a car. He risked my health by playing around with a hooker. He was sleeping with a seventeen-year-old girl. So okay, Columbo. I hired a private investigator to see just what was what and how far he'd gone. *She* came up with the names and numbers."

"Y' want to give me her name?"

"Margaret Simms."

"You made a good choice. If I ever needed a private detective, I'd think of Margaret Simms."

"Okay. I wanted to know what he was doing. Wouldn't any wife?"

"Sure," said Columbo sympathetically. "It's just one of those things a guy in my position has to find out."

4:59 P.M.

"Okay, you said when he focused on me," Ai-ling said grimly to Link. "The son of a bitch has *focused*. He's no dummy. He's figured out what we can't have him knowing."

They sat in the living room of Link's apartment. Ai-ling's legs were wide spread, maybe to encourage Link.

"What?"

"There are little things! I guess you can't do it without leaving little things screwed up. Little piece of glass where a little piece of glass shouldn't have been! Footprint on the carpet—of a bare foot. God knows what else! Link . . . We've got to lay the thing one hundred percent on Piers Karlsen, or I'm on my way!"

"How you figure you can plant the Buddha on Karlsen?"

"Can it be so damned difficult? We put it in his apartment. We put it in his car. Then we call—your voice, *you* call—and leave word where the thing can be found. I *told* you it would be a mistake to destroy it. It's our *salvation!*"

"*In* his apartment? *In* his car? How are we going to get into his apartment or his car?"

"For Christ's sake, Link! People enter other people's houses and cars all the time! It's just a matter of knowing how and having the tools."

"I don't know how, and I don't have the tools. What do you have?"

"*Use your brains!* If a subliterate burglar can— If he can do it, we can do it!"

"How?"

"Tools, Link. I've read that a man with the right tools and some know-how can open a car and drive off with it in the same amount of time the owner can drive off using the keys. We don't even have to jump-start the son of a bitch. All we need to do is open the door."

"I—"

"That's his car. Opening his apartment, which would be better, would be easier. Less likely an alarm, guy like Karlsen."

Link shook his head violently. "We'd be *amateurs!*"

"Dental picks, Link," she said. "We work on the locks here, we work on the locks at your place, till we learn how to do it. Hardware. *Get it, Link!* Buy it tomorrow. We don't have all the time in the world."

9:11 P.M.

Columbo was old enough to remember a place called Whisky à Go-go. He remembered The Body Shop. Some way, the innocent exuberance of places like that had faded. He was sorry that had happened. There was something odd about new attitudes.

This club was called The Store. Columbo looked around. No hookers were working the crowd, or if they were they were doing it very quietly. He saw two guys from the Vice Squad. They had to be there to see the show. They were there to have a good time. Those guys had a lot of good times.

They were a couple of mugs, thickset and a bit shabby. One was bald, and the other had a little sandy hair remaining on a pink pate that showed through. One of them recognized him and invited him to come to their table.

"Columbo, Homicide," the man said, introducing Columbo to the other Vice Squad man. "He's Joe."

"Nice to meet ya," said Columbo. "How's it goin', Mac?"

"Nothin' new, nothin' different. I'm puttin' in for a transfer to Narcotics. Like to get into Homicide, but you guys are an elite and won't let in peasants like us." Mac was sandy-haired; Joe was the bald one.

Columbo shrugged. "They let *me* in," he said.

"Columbo's modest," said Mac to Joe. "That's a little game he plays."

A waitress came, and Columbo ordered a beer.

"Here on business, Lieutenant?" Joe asked.

" 'Fraid so. Pamela Murphy, also known as Pamela Starr. Need to talk to her. You guys know her?"

Joe grinned. "Sure. You want her to come here to this table? She doesn't go on stage for half an hour or so yet."

"Y' mean she goes on about a quarter to ten?"

"Right."

"So she doesn't have to be here till . . . nine-thirty or so."

"Right."

"I'll go back and get her," said Mac.

"She any problem?" Columbo asked Joe. "I looked at her rap sheet. She was busted for shoplifting ten years ago, nothing since."

"She doesn't make waves, Columbo. We could find something to make her for if we wanted to be nasty, but what'd be the point?"

"You mean she goes home with the customers?"

"Now and then. She's not a hooker, Columbo—though maybe that depends on how you define it. Let's just say that she occasionally gets a proposition that interests her."

Columbo drank beer and watched a redheaded stripper work the stage. There was nothing new, he decided.

Mac returned, bringing Pamela Murphy. She was as Columbo had seen her at the funeral: tall, with dark hair piled high, dark eyed, wearing exaggerated makeup, probably already made up for the stage. She wore tight, knit black stirrup pants and a man's white, ribbed vest undershirt.

Columbo stood. She took his hand.

"So . . . Homicide. What can I do for you, Lieutenant?"

"Prob'ly nothin'. I just have to talk with people who knew Gunnar Svan."

"Well. I knew Gunnar Svan."

"Pretty well, too, huh? He gave you a nice car."

She nodded. "He gave me a nice car."

"Maybe Columbo's too polite to ask," said Joe, "but did Svan pay you?"

"You gonna make me?"

"C'mon, Pam."

"Okay. Yes, he did, at first. Then he gave me the car, and of course after that . . . You know."

"When'd you see him last?" Columbo asked.

"He called me and asked me to come out in the desert where he was shooting a flick."

"When was that?"

"It had to be on a Sunday, when this joint's closed."

"Was there a girl living with him? Seventeen years old?"

"She said she was eighteen. How'd you know?"

"I'm investigating the man's murder. So I know a lot of things."

"Did you and Svan and a seventeen-year-old girl make a threesome?" asked Mac.

"Hey, Mac! It happened in Arizona!"

Joe laughed. "Right. Outside our jurisdiction."

"Do you believe the Buddha was worth a million?" Columbo asked.

Pamela shrugged. "How would I know? It coulda been a piece of carnival glass for all I could tell."

"You did see it, then?"

"Right. I saw it a coupla times."

"Did he tell you how much it was worth?"

"He said a mill."

"He let you touch it?"

"I guess so. Why?"

"Your fingerprints might be on it, then?"

"Hey! What *is* this? You got it? My prints are on it?"

Columbo smiled weakly and turned up his hands. "I don't have it yet. But I'm lookin' for explanations for the fingerprints on it. I understand jade takes fingerprints very well. And of course you got a record for liftin' other people's property."

"Hey! You're hasslin' me! I was *here* when he got it. A hundred people saw me here."

"All of you," Mac said dryly.

"But you don't have to be here till nine-thirty," said Columbo. He sipped beer. "I haven't got anything on you, Miss Murphy. I don't think you killed Gunnar Svan. But I do want you to do me a favor. I want you to think it all through and see if there's not something you can tell me that might help me find out who did it. Any little thing. Any little fact. May not seem important to you. Might be important to me."

She nodded. "Can I go? I got a job here."

"Sure."

When she had left the table, Columbo spoke to the two men from Vice. "You guys can do me a favor, if you will. I need to know if she's got a special boyfriend."

"Got it, Columbo," said Mac. "We'll look into it and be in touch. Maybe if we help you break the Svan case, you could put in a word for me if I try to get a transfer to Homicide."

NINE

THURSDAY, AUGUST 6—9:34 A.M.

Sergeant Daniel Brittigan looked like a Marine drill
sergeant—which in fact he had once been. He had his uniforms tailored to fit his erect, muscular body, and he carried himself with rigid military bearing. He had been
wounded in the line of duty with LAPD and so had been
assigned to the police pistol range as range officer for the
few years remaining before he could retire on full pension.

He stared at the wheezing Peugeot that had pulled into
the parking lot. God help him, it was Lieutenant Columbo
again! Here he came, raincoat flapping in the wind, cigar
smoke trailing behind him, grinning as though he were
happy to be here. Where was his Beretta? Probably forgot
to bring it.

"Hiya, Brittigan. Guess what?"

"You got orders directly from the Chief to qualify with
your Beretta," said the sergeant. "I know. They copied
me."

Columbo turned down the corners of his mouth and nodded. "Yeah. The new gun. Y' know, Sarge, I got so I liked that old gun I had."

"The revolver."

"Yeah. I could look at it, and I could see if it had bullets in it. This one here, I can't tell if it's loaded or not. I pull the trigger, and does it go off or not? I can't tell. It's an odd gun, don't ya think?"

"Lieutenant, that Beretta is one of the finest handguns manufactured in the world."

"Yeah? Well, it seems odd to me. How come I can't see if it's got bullets in it or not? Or am I missin' somethin'? Has it got an *indicator* or somethin' on it? Y' see, mechanical things just defy me to understand them. Like, Mrs. Columbo won't let me use the dishwasher."

"It's a fine weapon, Lieutenant."

"If ya say so."

Having had no other way to carry the gun, since it would not fit in a raincoat pocket, Columbo had worn his shoulder holster for the first time since it was issued to him. Gingerly, he lifted the Beretta automatic out and stared skeptically at it. "How can I tell if it's loaded?"

"It's very simple, Lieutenant. Entirely simple. Let me show you."

Brittigan released and dropped the clip. It was loaded. He pulled the slide. The Beretta spat a cartridge over the side. It had been loaded.

"Y' see, Lieutenant? It *was* loaded. If you'd pulled the trigger—"

"Bam," said Columbo quietly. "That's what I was afraid of. How could you tell?"

"The way I just showed you. Press here and release the clip. Pull back the slide. It's not loaded now. It just ejected a cartridge."

The sergeant handed the Beretta back to Columbo. "Okay, pull the trigger," he said.

"You're sure—?"

"I'm sure. Point it up in the air and pull the trigger."

Columbo did. The automatic snapped sharply. The firing pin hit an empty chamber.

"See?"

"You were *sure?*"

"So completely sure I'd have let you point it at me and pull that trigger."

"No way, Sarge."

"Okay, let's get some rounds in and put some holes in a target," said Sergeant Brittigan. "It's more accurate than the revolver was, so you shouldn't have any trouble qualifying. Here's the clip. Shove it in."

Frowning intently, Columbo shoved the loaded clip into the slot in the grip.

"Alright. Now cock it."

"Cock it?"

"Pull the slide back and then let it go forward. That'll cock it."

Columbo glanced skeptically at Sergeant Brittigan but did as he was told. He pulled back the slide and released it.

The pistol fired. The shot went into the ground six inches from Columbo's left foot and not more than nine inches from Brittigan's.

The whole range fell silent as twenty officers stared.

Brittigan's face was white. "You don't hold the trigger in while you're cocking the pistol, Lieutenant," he said coldly.

"Y' didn't tell me that."

Brittigan stared at the scar the bullet had made in the ground, halfway between their feet. "I'm going to send the

Chief a special recommendation that you be allowed to carry your old revolver, Lieutenant Columbo. With an automatic, you're going to *kill somebody!*"

Columbo nodded. "That's what I said all along. Mechanical stuff—"

10:10 A.M.

Dental picks would not do it. Damn! Link had furnished a set, but they were too delicate, too ready to bend. Picking a lock required something more substantial. Picking a lock was not, in fact, going to be easy.

Ai-ling had read there wasn't any lock that couldn't be picked, but now she learned there was something more to it. Apparently picking a lock took some degree of . . . talent? Or practice. Maybe it was practice that counted.

Ai-ling sat down in a chair beside her own front door and worked on the lock with the dental picks. She worked and worked. Bend? After all, lock tumblers didn't require major force; they turned easily enough with a key. She could feel tumblers moving, but it wasn't enough apparently just to move them out of the way; some had to be moved one way, some another. Maybe the ease with which locks could be picked was a myth. Lock manufacturers, after all, had to have *some* little ingenuity.

She had run an article in *Glitz* two or three years ago about how burglars entered the homes of the rich and famous. Often they used a tool called a slaphammer. It was a hard steel probe, like a key, that went into the key channel of a lock and then was struck with a heavy lead weight.

It simply destroyed the tumblers in the lock, which could then be opened rather simply. No good. It left spectacular evidence that the premises had been violated.

Damnit! If she could just plant the Buddha—

In his car. That would be easier. She'd read, she'd heard, about car thieves who could enter an automobile and jump-start it in less time than it took for the owner to open and start it with a key.

How the hell did they do that? She was not totally ignorant of how. She went to the garage and looked at her car. (Gunnar's was gone, towed away by the police for some imponderable reason.) The window slid up into a rubber slot, which sealed it against rain and splashes. A thin metal tool, inserted between the rubber and the glass, could reach the latch handle and pry it out. Once again, matter of the right tool and some practice. She began to search the garage and the basement. If she couldn't find the right tool, maybe Link could.

3

11:13 A.M.

"Hiya, Pavlov."

The civilian technician from the Crime Scene Unit smiled and shook her head. "The name's Jean, Lieutenant. Odd name with Pavlov, maybe—maybe I should have been Olga or Tatiana or something—but it's what my parents called me."

"I'm always slow to call people by their first names," said Columbo. "Women, especially. I don't want to seem too familiar."

"Columbo— If we're going to talk about semen and pubic hair, we can hardly go on being formal."

"Uhh . . . I guess so."

"We found what you were looking for. There were drops of semen on the front seat of Gunnar Svan's Mercedes. Also hair, some long and straight, some short and curly. The curly hair looks for all the world like pubic hair. We've sent the semen samples to the DNA lab in Sacramento to see if it came from Svan. The hair—" She shrugged.

"I can maybe help you out on that, Jean. When I interviewed Miss Karlsen, I asked her for some strands of hair. She jerked them out. I—" He reached into his raincoat pocket and pulled out a folded sheet of paper, which he opened to disclose the strands of hair. "Sorry— Guess I should have turned those in to the evidence room. But hair—"

"Hair doesn't change, Lieutenant. It would have been nice to have a better evidence track."

"I hope the case doesn't turn on whether or not the hair found in Svan's car was Miss Karlsen's," said Columbo. "I hope we'll have a stronger case than that. I mean, like— Okay, she had sex with him in his car. We're not trying to prove that. Or even when. But it'd be useful to know if she did or didn't. Just useful. Not vital."

4

1:30 P.M.

Margaret Simms kept no fancy office. Columbo could understand that. She'd be out most of the time doing legwork, as he was. But she did have a fancy-looking computer on her credenza. He wondered what she used it for.

She was an exceptionally tall woman, and slender. Her hair was gray, but it was obviously styled by a hairdresser, and her makeup had maybe been designed by a cosmetician. She was stylish, in Columbo's judgment. This afternoon she was wearing tapered gray slacks and a loose white knit shirt.

"The work I do for a client is confidential, of course," she said.

He smiled and shook his head. "Not from me it isn't. I'm sure you know the law. Doctors can keep secrets from the police. Lawyers can. Priests. But not private investigators."

She returned his smile. "You can't blame me for trying."

"I don't. But I gotta ask you some questions. Your client knows I'm talking to you. She's where I got your name."

"Mrs. Cooper-Svan."

"Right."

Margaret Simms sighed. "Well, I suppose I've got no choice. What you want to know?"

"To start with, when did Mrs. Cooper-Svan hire you?"

"July sixth."

"What did she want you to do?"

"She wanted me to find out what women Mr. Svan was seeing. She knew about Pamela Murphy and about the car he gave her, but she suspected there were others. I sent a paparazzo to Arizona with a big telephoto lens. He got good, clear pictures of two more women and the license plates on their cars."

"Which made it possible for you to find out who they were."

Margaret Simms nodded.

"The question I have to think about is this: Did one of these women have a friend that might have killed Mr.

Svan to get the million-dollar Buddha? I mean, maybe one of them went to the house, saw the Buddha, was told what it was and what it was worth, and set up a deal to— Ya get my drift? So how did you find out that Muriel Paul's a hooker?"

"Her license plates identified her. Then I checked her rap sheet. I checked Pamela Murphy's, too."

"Did you find out anything about their friends?"

"No. My job was to find out if Gunnar Svan was hosting women in his trailer and if so, who."

"Those women were in Svan's house and saw the Buddha," said Columbo. "I—"

Margaret Simms shook her head. "Eliminate Ingrid Karlsen. I don't think she ever met Gunnar Svan before she went to Arizona to 'audition' for him."

"Had to," said Columbo. "How else she come to know him? How else she get an audition? She didn't have an agent, did she?"

"I'd rather think she had a pimp."

Columbo grinned. "Now, now."

"Okay. She shows up in the middle of the Arizona desert, driving an almost new Toyota—a rented car, incidentally. How does this kid get admitted to Gunnar Svan's director's trailer? Half the good-lookin' girls in LA would have liked to be there. But they don't get into Svan's bed. *She* does. Who arranged that?"

"Got any ideas?"

"No. Has it got anything to do with his murder?"

"I'm not sure."

Margaret Simms leaned back in her chair and lit a cigarette. "Smoke a cigar, Columbo," she said. "I understand you do."

"I try to be a gentleman about it."

"My involvement in the lives of Gunnar Svan and Eileen

Cooper-Svan was a matter of adultery," she said. "That's my stock in trade, Columbo: wandering husbands and wives, plus the California community property law. Murder is *your* business, not mine. Thank god."

"Yours once, if I remember. Uh . . . Got a match? I mean, didn't Felicio murder his wife because of what you found out about her?"

"Are you suggesting that my report to Mrs. Cooper-Svan drove her to murder her husband?"

"No. But I do got to wonder. Three weeks after you are hired to look into the fun and games played by Gunnar Svan, Gunnar Svan is dead, murdered."

"Hey, really! Do you think Mrs. Cooper-Svan killed him? Or had him killed?"

Columbo used her lighter to touch fire to the tip of a cigar that had been only about one-quarter smoked before. "I don't figure that. It's just one of the facts of the case."

"Columbo, what the hell you want to know?"

"When she hired you to look into what women he was seeing, did she ask you to look into anything else?"

"No."

"So all you know is that she wanted to find out if he was straying from the marriage?"

"That's it. And if so, with who."

"Nothing more?"

"No, that's it. She was an aggrieved wife."

"Well— One more little thing, if you don't mind. I mean, I'm takin' up a lot of your time. But, I do have one more little question. You get any impression from her that his . . . his, uh, adventures with other women was the total of it? Or was she concerned about something else?"

"Like—?"

"Like the way he spent money."

"Okay. Okay, Columbo, you hit it maybe. She didn't like

the way he'd given Pamela Murphy a $60,000 car, and she was interested in how much he might have given others. I got the idea she was having a close look at the books."

"Was he *stealin'* from her?"

"I wouldn't be surprised. Like I said, I wasn't hired to look into anything like that; but when you work on a matter, you do get certain impressions. I couldn't testify."

"Thank ya, Ms. Simms. That's kind of a new approach to the case."

5:45 P.M.

When Columbo pulled his Peugeot into his driveway, Mrs. Columbo's car was not there. Nothing unusual. She was not expecting him before six or six-thirty and had probably gone shopping.

Dog wasn't in the house. Where could he be? Mrs. Columbo never took him with her when she went shopping. Columbo stepped out the back door and looked around the yard. Then he had an idea. He walked over to the hedge that separated his lot from his neighbors'. And there was Dog. The old basset hound was leisurely paddling around in the neighbors' swimming pool.

"Hiya, Nell. Sorry about that."

"No problem, Columbo. Glad to have him."

Nell Finch was Bob Finch's wife. She was stretched out on an aluminum-and-webbing chaise longue, taking the sun. She was a woman of forty-five or so and looked handsome in her yellow bikini.

"I don't want him to make a nuisance of himself."

"He doesn't. I think he's cute. Want a beer?"

"Sounds good." He walked around the end of the hedge.

Dog spotted him and clambered out of the pool, wagging his tail. He ran toward his master and just before he reached him stopped to shake.

Nell laughed.

"That's why I wear a raincoat when it's not raining. Ya never know."

She pulled a can of beer from a Styrofoam ice chest. "I suppose the old boy gets hot and wants to cool off," she said, nodding at Dog.

"I'm afraid I got a different idea," said Columbo. "I figure he wants to drown his fleas."

"Has Dog got fleas?"

"Is he a dog? Yeah, he's got fleas. I dust him once in a while. It's like askin' if he'll bite, which somebody does ask now and again. I never knew him to bite, but suppose he would if he wanted to. He's a dog."

TEN

FRIDAY, AUGUST 7—8:23 A.M.

Columbo checked in at headquarters. He found a note on his desk saying Captain Sczciegel wanted to see him immediately. He went to the captain's office.

"Columbo— What the hell did you do, try to kill Sergeant Brittigan?"

"Big problem with that gun, Captain. I told ya it wasn't safe."

The captain picked up a sheet of paper and slapped it. "This is a special order from the Chief, exempting you from carrying a Beretta. But, Columbo, you gotta *carry* your revolver. That's an order." Captain Sczciegel reached in his desk drawer and pulled out the snubnose .38 revolver Columbo had kept in his hall closet for so many years. It was in a new nylon holster. "Now. Take off your raincoat. Take off your jacket."

Shaking his head, looking worried, Columbo took off the raincoat and jacket. Captain Sczciegel helped him strap on the shoulder holster.

"Looks familiar," Columbo said as he took the revolver in his hand.

The captain handed him a box of cartridges. "Load it, Columbo."

"Well, maybe I—"

"*Load it,* Columbo!"

Columbo frowned as he inserted six cartridges in the chambers of the revolver. "Makes me uneasy," he said. "Y' know, I've never needed to shoot."

"Set the safety."

"That's this thing here?"

"That's that thing there. In order to fire it, you've gotta push that back to where it was before. Is that so difficult?"

"Well, at least when I look at this gun I can see it's got bullets in it."

"Right. Now shove it down in your holster. *Not with your finger on the trigger!* You don't put your finger on the trigger unless you're going to fire."

"I thought the safety—"

"Right. Even so, keep your finger off the trigger when you're loading or putting the pistol in your holster. Remember that, Columbo!"

"Awright."

"Okay. Now, Lieutenant Columbo, you look like a police officer. Or would if you'd learn to tie your neckties right. And maybe got a new raincoat—though I know it's useless for me to suggest it."

Columbo pulled on his jacket. He carried his raincoat. Uncomfortably, he stared down into his left armpit. He shook his head. "Okay, Cap'n, but it sure feels funny."

He'd noticed the other note on his desk, saying Mac from Vice wanted to see him. In the elevator on his way to the Vice Squad offices, Columbo felt certain people were staring at what seemed to him had to be a conspicuous bulge in his armpit. He'd seen other kinds of holsters. He could carry the gun on his right hip, where it would be under the loose part of his jackets. Some guys even carried them strapped to their ankles, out of sight inside their pants legs—though they couldn't do that with the Berettas. If he had to carry this thing, maybe he'd find some other kind of holster, not too obvious.

Mac was waiting for him. "Hey, Columbo! Want to recommend me for a transfer to Homicide? I got somethin' for ya."

"Whatcha got, ol' buddy?"

"Coffee?"

"If it's as bad coffee as what we get in Homicide, I don't know."

"It's not. We take up a collection and rent a coffeemaker, with supplies. We can just step in the canteen back there. C'mon."

As they walked back to the canteen, they passed a bench where a tearful young woman in a tight red sweater and a short black vinyl skirt sat with her left hand cuffed to a chain that was attached to a ring in the wall.

"Madge . . . Not *you* again! What's it this time? Won't you ever—?"

"Same ol' shit," she sobbed. "You guys never let up."

"Why don't *you* try lettin' up?"

Mac walked on. When they were beyond the young woman's hearing, he turned to Columbo and said, "Not your plain vanilla hooker. She's got a boyfriend that mugs her johns. This time she's off to Fontera, I expect. She knows it, too. That's why the boo-hoo."

In the canteen, Mac poured two paper cups of coffee. He stirred milk and sugar into his. "I did a little checking on Pam Murphy," he said. "The girl has certain connections. She's got a quiet little business. Bunko Squad has been watching her for several months. The way she works it is this— Her friends tip her off when the right sucker comes in The Store. The right sucker is a guy, local or out-of-towner, who can't afford to have it known that he spent a night with an LA stripper. She concentrates on him when she's doing her act, and afterward she goes to him and says she noticed how interested he was. Can she sit down? She'll buy her own drink; she's not *that* kind of girl. She lets the guy make the proposition. She never suggests it. I mean, if an undercover Vice guy sat down with her, he couldn't make her. She's too clever. If the john suggests somethin', she plays coy at first, then says, well, seeing what a nice guy he is . . . While she's alone with him, she gets his name and address and phone number. In the morning she says it'd be a good idea if he'd send her some money. How much? Well . . . two or three thousand ought to take care of her."

"Did she do the same thing to Gunnar Svan? Is that how she got the BMW out of him?"

"No. He was her sugar daddy. She also arranged 'entertainment' for him. Other girls. Even boys."

"What about Muriel Paul? Does she work the same scam?"

"I doubt it. Muriel's a streetwalker. Gunnar was a

cruiser. I imagine he saw her, picked her up, and—"

"But one of Pam's guys could have killed Gunnar, for the jade Buddha."

Mac nodded. "Right. Could have. I hope the info is useful for you."

"The interestin' question," said Columbo, "is, who are these friends that finger suckers for her?"

"Not a very nice guy," said Mac. "Remember Jacky Di Giacomo?"

Columbo's head snapped up. "You bet I do."

"You had him made for Murder One. Had it good on him. So what pops up at trial but a pretty, demure little schoolteacher who testified with shy blushes that at the time when Mr. Di Giacomo was supposed to be killing a man in Bel Air, he was in fact in bed with *her,* in a Malibu motel. That was the closest we ever came to getting Jacky. He's done short sentences for this and that but never the big time he had coming."

"Made me look like an idiot," said Columbo.

"No. Everybody understood but the jury. The lawyers took care of that. Everybody understood but the jury."

"Often the case," Columbo said quietly.

3

10:28 A.M.

Ai-ling sat behind her desk. Adrienne faced her.

Sitting to one side was Gilbert Gleason, the man who had photographed Adrienne. If the women could have read his mind they would have known he was thinking what a privilege it would be to be able to photograph them together. He had photographed them separately, but to-gether—

Each was, in her own distinctive way, a supremely beautiful woman.

Adrienne thought green complemented her red hair and often wore green. She was right. She was stunning, he thought, in her knit golf shirt and her pale-yellow stirrup pants. She had not been stunning nude. Her beauty had been more subtle—classic.

Ai-ling wore a loose, cream-white dress and sat in her habitual legs-apart posture. She was more urbane than Adrienne. Her soft, rounded features contrasted with Adrienne's more fine-cut ones. There was about her an understated effect that the redhead didn't aspire to.

Ai-ling had called Adrienne in to look at the photographs Gleason had taken Monday. Of the 150 exposures he and his assistant had made, he had selected forty to show to Ai-ling. Of those, she had rejected a dozen. The rest were now in a portfolio on Ai-ling's desk, to be shown to Adrienne.

"You are going to be proud of these," Ai-ling said. She began to take them from the portfolio, one by one, and lay them before Adrienne on the desk.

"My god!" whispered Adrienne.

Ai-ling smiled. "If you have a boyfriend who can't appreciate those, then you need a new boyfriend."

After Adrienne had seen all the photos, Ai-ling and Gleason set up six little easels on the desk and mounted six eight-by-ten prints.

"Those are the ones I want to publish."

Adrienne grinned nervously. "They leave nothing to the imagination, do they?"

"Oh, *a great deal,* Adrienne! A great deal."

"Well . . . I suppose so. You want me to agree to those six?"

"I—" Ai-ling was interrupted by a buzz on her telephone. "I left strict orders I wouldn't take any calls. This has got to be something. Excuse me." She lifted the telephone. "Tell him he'll have to wait a few minutes." She put down the phone. "You won't believe the coincidence," she said. "Lieutenant Columbo is outside."

"I was supposed to see him for lunch anyway," said Adrienne.

"We'll put the pictures out of sight."

Adrienne shrugged. "Why do that? If the whole world is going to see those six next month, why not let Columbo see them? He's a good friend. If I'm not going to be embarrassed when the pictures are published, why should I be embarrassed to have him see them now?"

Ai-ling raised her chin. "Your choice," she said.

Adrienne shrugged.

Columbo came in, spotted the photographs, and turned his eyes away. "Hey, I'm sorry. I—"

"Look at them, Columbo," said Adrienne. "There'll be millions of copies of them everywhere in a few weeks. October issue. Out sometime in September, right, Eileen?"

"Right. And please call me Ai-ling, Adrienne."

He looked at the photographs. He shifted his eyes to Adrienne, then back to the pictures, then to her again. "Well, they're good likenesses, I'll say that."

"This is Gilbert Gleason, the photographer who took them," said Ai-ling.

"I'd say you got a very interestin' line of work, Mr. Gleason."

"It is a very, very rewarding line of work," Gleason said gravely.

Columbo stared at the color prints and nodded. "Right. Rewarding." He turned to Ai-ling. "I guess I came at an awkward time."

"No. We were finished. We've chosen the pictures we'll use."

"Well I— I just had one or two little questions."

"Tell you what, Lieutenant. You and Adrienne are having lunch, I understand. Why don't you let me barge in? We'll talk off the record one hundred percent, but a part of the Adrienne Boswell story that will be published in *Glitz* will be her friendship with the famous Lieutenant Columbo of LAPD Homicide."

"I'm not sure—"

"C'mon, Columbo," said Adrienne. "Why not? We're all friends."

11:10 A.M.

Lunch would be at 12:30 at the Pacifica Club. Columbo had time to look up Martha Zimmer and see if she'd made any progress in looking into what friends Muriel Paul had. Again, he hailed a black-and-white and used its radio to contact Martha. She met him at the corner of Sunset and Courtney. He got in her car, and they talked.

"Hey, Columbo! You're packin' your piece! We're going to make a cop of you yet."

He glanced at his left armpit, at the revolver riding in its holster. "Yeah. Orders. If the thing was made of neon tubes it wouldn't be more conspicuous."

"Makes you a real policeman," she said.

"Yeah, I suppose. When I first came on The Job, back in NY, I walked a beat as a uniformed guy, and I had to carry my sidearm right out in plain sight. Y' know somethin'? I never fired a shot. Ninety percent or more of cops never fire a shot. Then I got to be a detective, and the thing didn't fit under my clothes right."

Martha chuckled. "Hey, Columbo. Where I'm lucky is, guys don't look for my gun. They stare at somethin' else first." She pointed at her generous breasts. "They just overlook the gun."

"Sure," said Columbo, half embarrassed. "Hey, I wondered if you found out anything about what kind of friends Muriel Paul has."

"Somebody who could steal a jade Buddha, or fence it?"

"Somethin' like that."

Martha shrugged. "I've had a tail on her since you asked me. She turned one trick, just one, since then. Far as I can figure out, she's a loner. No pimp. No close friends."

"Keep an eye on her."

12:30 P.M.

Columbo was on time, and Adrienne and Ai-ling were a little early. They sat at an outdoor table overlooking the swimming pool. Ai-ling was smoking and had a margarita before her.

"Columbo," said Adrienne with a degree of impatience. "Put the raincoat on the chair. You won't need any hardboiled eggs for a while."

"Okay. Hi there, Mrs. Cooper-Svan."

"Hello, Lieutenant. You too can call me Ai-ling."

" 'Kay. My, this is some elegant place! I'll tell Mrs. Columbo I had lunch here."

Adrienne looked quizzically at him. "Columbo," she said. "What the hell are you doing? Hey, man, you've got a *gun* in your armpit!"

"They made a big fuss about it. I'm supposed to carry it at all times. I'll be lucky I don't blow my foot off—which I almost did at the police range the other day. Anyway, I gotta carry the thing, they say; and that's somethin' else I got in my raincoat pocket: bullets."

Adrienne smiled at Ai-ling. "I believe he holds the LAPD record for having gone the longest time of any officer on the force without qualifying with his sidearm."

Columbo grinned and ran a hand through his tousled hair. "Never had reason to shoot anybody," he said. "Never had reason to point a gun at anybody. And if I did, I might point the wrong end. I don't figure guns do much good. Besides, I don't have any particular talent for handlin' 'em."

"Lieutenant," said Ai-ling, "I imagine you have some questions you want to ask me. So far as I'm concerned, you can ask them in front of Adrienne. She and I have become very good friends. And she, of course, is bound by journalistic ethics."

"Journalistic . . . Yeah. Well, I trust Adrienne for other reasons."

"Anyway, you did have questions?"

"Well, maybe one or two. The jade Buddha. That was yours, Mrs. Cooper-Svan? Not your husband's?"

Ai-ling nodded. "My great-great-grandfather earned most of the family fortune in China. The Coopers were shipowners and go back to the days of the clippers. They shipped tea and silk, among other things, from China to the States. Also coolies, I'm afraid—to build railroads. In the next generation, my great-grandfather married a Chinese girl. I'm named for her. He carried his bride—the first Ai-ling Cooper—wherever he went: China, India, around the Cape of Good Hope and up to London, then to Boston, then around Cape Horn to San Francisco and across the Pacific to Honolulu and back to Canton, and so on. They lived in the owner's cabin on a coal-burning steamship, and the family tradition—which of course I can't confirm—has it that he kept her in a chastity belt to protect her against the seamen. The tradition also is that she had bound feet. Anyway, they were married in 1894, and the Buddha came with her as part of her dowry. It has been passed down in the family from woman to woman. My grandmother, incidentally, was Chinese, too. When my mother died in 1986, the Buddha became mine."

"The million-dollar appraisal—?"

"That's how the insurance company appraised it and how they charged me premiums."

"Have you put in an insurance claim?"

Ai-ling was lighting another cigarette and did not answer until she finished. "Not yet. I notified the company of the loss, but I'm hoping you will recover it. It's worth more to me, you understand, than the money."

"I understand," said Columbo, "that you knew—"

He paused as a waiter stopped at their table and took his order for a Scotch and soda.

"I understand you knew that Pamela Murphy and Muriel Paul visited your house and saw the Buddha."

"That's right."

"How did you know that, Ma'am?"

"I didn't know their names. I found out who they were only after Margaret Simms identified them for me. Otherwise, it was easy enough, Lieutenant Columbo. Gunnar was an arrogant man. He supposed he had every right to carry on any way he wanted to, even to bring his chippies home, so long as I wasn't there. I smelled their perfume on my own bedsheets. I found my pillowcases stained with

Pamela Starr's hair dye. I didn't know the significance of it at the time, but I found in the kitchen one day a half-eaten box of doughnuts, printed JUST DONUTS. The doughnut girl was a *whore,* Lieutenant!" Ai-ling snorted. "For that matter, what would you call Pamela Starr?"

"How did you find out that he'd bought her an expensive car?"

"Simple enough. He didn't have any money of his own. He had a checking account, but I had to make deposits to it."

"Was he stealing from you?"

"What would you call it, buying a sixty-thousand-dollar car for a stripteaser?"

"I mean, worse than that."

Ai-ling shrugged. "I don't know. I haven't gone through his accounts yet."

Columbo nodded. "I can understand. It's only been a week."

Ai-ling pushed back her chair. "You'll have to excuse me," she said. "Call of nature."

Adrienne watched Ai-ling walk into the club, to the bathrooms. "Columbo," she said, "if I didn't know better, I'd think you suspect Ai-ling killed Gunnar."

Columbo shrugged. "I have to think along those lines. When there's murder, you have to think about husbands and wives."

"He was cheating on her, but she still loved him. I'm sure of it."

"Maybe so."

"Not maybe so. It's so. You may be embarrassed to ask her, but I'm not. I'll ask her."

Columbo shrugged. "Do they have good seafood here?"

Ai-ling returned, sat down, and lit a cigarette. "I'm for another drink before we order," she said.

"Ai-ling," said Adrienne. "I want to ask you a personal question. I want Columbo to hear the answer."

Ai-ling shrugged.

"Gunnar was cheating on you. But how were things between you, even so?"

"Meaning—?"

"Meaning, did you still love him? Meaning . . . were you still *intimate?*"

Ai-ling glanced at Columbo, then back at Adrienne, then at Columbo again. "Okay," she said quietly. "Gunnar— The reason Gunnar had so many women was, he was a *stallion!* Yes, he played around. But he came back to me. We had something more." She paused, sighed. "Alright, I'll tell you something. The night he . . . died. I've told you, Lieutenant, he got drunk. But before he got drunk— Lieutenant Columbo . . . Adrienne . . . Gunnar made love to me like only he could. I mean, it was everything. Complete. I couldn't have asked for any more. When I saw you for dinner, Adrienne, I was exhausted."

Columbo nodded soberly. "Well that, uh . . . That's interestin', Mrs. Cooper-Svan. I'm very sorry we have to go into anything like that. That's private sort of stuff."

Ai-ling nodded. " 'T's alright, Columbo. When there's been murder, people lose their privacy. For a while, anyway."

ELEVEN

1

Ai-ling wore black: a black watch cap, black sweat-shirt, black slacks, black shoes. Maybe that was being dramatic, but maybe it would make her more difficult to see in the night. Link had argued that a figure dressed entirely in black *looked* like somebody on an evil errand, who would arouse suspicion at first sight. Well— There was more to it than that. Anyone who got a good look at her would spot the latex gloves, too.

Anyway, she hadn't brought along a mask.

On the other hand, in her black leather shoulder bag she was carrying a 9-mm Glock, a deadly automatic pistol. Caught in the posture of a sneak thief, with the jade Buddha in her possession, she would be on her way to the gas chamber, to life in prison at the very least. If confronted, she would shoot. She couldn't be in any worse trouble.

The Buddha was in a small brown paper grocery sack, down in the shoulder bag with the pistol and her car keys. The tool she hoped would give her quick and easy access

---

to Karlsen's old Chevy was inside her slacks. She had shoved it down her left leg, where it ran from her waistband almost to her knee. She walked stiffly, holding the tool against her leg with her left hand.

She felt certain the long narrow steel blade would open the Chevy. It opened Link's Cadillac. It opened her Jaguar. It was nothing more complicated than the blade of an old sword her great-grandfather had worn as part of his uniform as a Knight Templar. She had used a hammer to break off the pointed tip, so as not to cut the rubber seal of a car door and leave a mark that would say the car had been broken into. With the hammer she had broken the blade in two, giving her a tool about sixteen inches long. She had practiced for an hour on the Jaguar and Cadillac and was certain she could open the Chevrolet. She had checked out the Chevy that afternoon, where it was parked on the street close to Karlsen's photofinishing shop. She had seen nothing about it that looked as if it would be more difficult to open than the Cadillac. The lock handle looked very similar.

She knew where to find the car. It was parked in the lot behind the apartment building where Piers Karlsen and his daughter lived. She had driven by to be sure.

Her Jaguar was parked two blocks away, on a dark street. It was an eminently stealable automobile, a favorite among professional auto thieves, and she had locked The Club on the steering wheel before she left it.

The parking lot was lighted, unfortunately. Ai-ling pulled the blade from her slacks, crouched in the shadow of a Dumpster, and checked out the area. None but night-lights burned in the windows of the apartments. No one was making love in any of the parked cars.

She watched for a while, but sooner or later she would have to move. She moved. She slipped between Karlsen's

Chevy and a Toyota that was parked next to it. She examined the Chevy again, looking for a window sticker that would say it was equipped with an alarm system. Maybe it had one but had no sticker to announce it. *That* would be a nasty surprise.

She glanced around once more, then moved to the front of the driver's-side door. As quickly as she could, she inserted the blade between the rubber seal and the glass. It went through easily. Now she was glad the parking lot was lighted. Peering through the corner of the windshield, she manipulated the blade under the latch handle. She twisted.

Damn! The blade slipped out and did not move the handle.

Her mouth was dry and her hands trembled as she tried again. The blade slipped. It didn't wedge between the handle and the plastic panel behind the recess. She put the palm of her left hand on the end of the blade and pushed down as hard as she could. Then she pried.

Damn! It worked!

She pulled the outside handle. The door opened. She checked the inside handle and the plastic around it to be sure she hadn't scratched it. If she had, the deal was off; she would take the Buddha and scram. But she'd made no scratches.

She found the trunk-latch release and lifted it. The rear lid boomped and rose an inch. She stepped to the rear of the Chevy, lifted the lid, and shoved the sack containing the Buddha into the spare-tire well. She closed the lid, returned to the door, locked it and closed it.

The job was done!

2

3:09 A.M.

Her Jaguar was painted British racing green. She had owned it four years and was proud of it. Walking into the street where she had parked it, Ai-ling was all but ebullient. This thing had worked out great. So far.

But— A man was tampering with her car! He was working at the door. He had a tool not very different from her blade. Obviously he could see The Club on her steering wheel, so apparently he knew how to defeat it. Opening the car as he was about to do, he would set off a screeching alarm.

She dropped the blade and pulled the Glock from her bag.

She could not think rationally without more time. All she could think of was—when the man opened the car, the alarm would go off. He might go driving through the streets with the alarm hooting. He might be an addict, stealing a car to buy a few fixes. If he were caught and told where he found it, that would place her car within two blocks of Piers Karlsen's apartment—at three in the morning!

"Hey! Get away from my car!"

The man turned toward her. "*Your* car? My car, Sis. I saw it first."

The man was a huge black. The light caught the whites of his eyes. She could not judge, but she guessed he was strung out on something. He didn't quite focus on her, if she was right. He didn't see the gun in her hand.

"It's my car, Mister. Back off it. Go steal somebody else's."

So far he had apparently regarded her as a nuisance. Now he filled with breath and seemed to expand. "No, Sis," he growled. He moved toward her.

Ai-ling fired. The man grunted and hesitated but was only a little slowed in coming at her. She fired again.

"Sis . . . Why you want hurt Ed?" He clutched his belly and groaned. "You *kill* Ed!"

She fired a third time. He fell forward, and his head struck the pavement and broke like a melon dropped on concrete.

Ai-ling ran around him, unlocked her car, unlocked The Club, and started the car. Lights were coming on in houses on the street, and her tires screeched as she pulled around the body and sped away.

Christ Jesus! She'd left the blade!

Well . . . It had no fingerprints on it.

3:50 A.M.

Someday when she sold the house she would have to retrieve the Glock and eliminate any chance it would ever be found by a subsequent owner. For now, she knew where it would be safe. There was a fireplace in the living room. No wood had been burned in it for many years. It was equipped with gas logs, ghastly things, and she had almost never lighted them, though Gunnar sometimes had. Under the logs was a trapdoor. When wood was burned, the ashes could be disposed of by shoving the trapdoor open with the poker and sweeping the ashes into the opening. The ashes fell down a chute. At the bottom of the chute a door opened, and the ashes could be shoveled out and hauled away. She had checked the chute. Some ashes remained there, maybe a foot or two of them. Tonight, she shoved the Glock through the trapdoor. She heard it hit the soft ashes in the chute. Down in there, it would never be found, so long as she owned the house.

Anyway, no one would be looking for it. It had been Gunnar's.

She ran the latex gloves through the disposal and cleaned the disposal by running potatoes and ice cubes through, as she had done before.

Now she changed her clothes and drove to Link's apartment.

6:54 A.M.

That it was Saturday made no difference to Bobby Wilson. He had newspapers to deliver, and people expected their *Times* before they left for work in the morning. Some of the people on his route worked on Saturdays and wanted their papers as early that day as on any other day.

He rode his bicycle and tossed the papers onto door stoops. He'd done it for two years and knew just how to throw.

It was going to be a smoggy day. The sun was red. The whole world was red. He turned a corner. Something strange: two police cars sat on the street. Two men were walking around, measuring with a tape, making notes in a notebook. A woman was taking pictures. A cop in uniform stood beside a black-and-white with flashing lights.

He had papers to deliver, just the same. And he missed one. Annoyed, he kicked down his kickstand and walked up to the bushes where the paper had landed. He retrieved it and tossed it on the stoop. As he walked back to his bicycle he noticed something lying in the grass between the sidewalk and the street. What? It looked like the blade of an old sword, broken at both ends.

He didn't touch it. He tossed two more newspapers and then reached the police car. "What's up?" he asked the man in uniform.

"A man was shot and killed here during the night. Right there."

Bobby saw the huge bloodstain on the pavement. His stomach churned. "Uh— I don't know if it means anything, but there's an old sword blade in the grass right over there."

"Yeah?" The officer turned to one of the plainclothes officers. "Hey, Jean. The boy here says there's an old sword blade in the grass over there."

Jean Pavlov of the Crime Scene Unit put a lens cap on her camera. "Show me," she said.

8:37 A.M.

Ai-ling stood outside the telephone booth and listened to Link calling police headquarters.

Link tried to mimic a British accent. "Yes. I need to speak with a leftenant— I believe his name is Columbo. Of course. I will hold."

He turned and looked at Ai-ling. She stood outside the booth, smoking a cigarette.

Link didn't know she had killed the man who was trying to steal her car. It wasn't necessary for Link to know everything. He didn't have what you could call nerves of steel.

"I see. He won't be in today. Well, p'raps you can take a message for him. Or p'raps someone else will be interested in why I'm calling. You see, someone tried yesterday to sell me a jade figurine of the Buddha. 'Twas worth a great deal of money, he said. But I'd read that such a figurine was stolen in the murder of Mr. Gunnar Svan. Naturally I wasn't interested in it. Sure path to the nick. Which the bahstard who tried to sell it to me well knew. I cahn't really like people who try to do that sort of thing to a fellow. Anyway— 'Twas in a brown paper bag in the boot of his automobile. A Mr. Piers Karlsen. Must ring off. Cahn't stay on the line. That's my information for the leftenant."

6

9:03 A.M.

Ai-ling told Link she wanted ham and eggs for breakfast. He didn't have any ham in his refrigerator, so she said she'd go to a market and get some, plus some cigarettes. He said he'd go with her. She said no, she'd rather he took a shower and get a fresh pot of coffee going. Since the Jag was low on gas, did he mind if she drove his Cadillac?

She drove fast through the morning smog, hoping she wouldn't be stopped and get a ticket. She arrived on the street where she shot the man. She stopped where she'd dropped the blade. Damn! It wasn't there.

Well— It had no fingerprints on it.

10:43 A.M.

Wearily, impatiently, Columbo strapped on the shoulder holster and shoved the revolver down in it. He was going to headquarters and might run into the captain. Better to have the gun on his person. The captain was a demon about it right now.

This was supposed to be his day off. But the dispatcher had called. On a tip they had found the jade Buddha.

That is to say, Martha Zimmer had found it. It was supposed to be in the trunk of Piers Karlsen's car; and, sure enough, there she'd found it. She'd sent two uniformed officers to arrest Piers Karlsen, and he was in custody.

Dog didn't bite him. Dog, though, had been enjoying a romp on the beach when Mrs. Columbo arrived and brought word of the call from the dispatcher. Columbo had asked her to stay with Dog and let him chase seagulls for a while. She had agreed and had stayed, but Columbo knew that Dog regarded Mrs. Columbo with a degree of scorn as an insufficiently appreciative observer of efforts to catch gulls. His master encouraged him. The woman just watched with condescending smiles. Dog knew the difference. He had barked angrily when Columbo strode up the beach to the car. Columbo wasn't sure who he felt sorrier for: Dog or himself. Or maybe poor Mrs. C, who had to walk on the beach with an unappreciative dog.

The Buddha . . . There was something wrong about this. It was too pat, too easy. More than a week after the murder of Gunnar Svan, a suspect had the hottest piece of hot property in the country in the trunk of his car?

At headquarters he listened to the taped telephone call for "Leftenant Columbo" before he went to talk to Karlsen.

"What could I do?" Martha asked. "What choice did anybody have? What would you have done, Columbo? Wouldn't you have had him collared?"

"Y' did right, Martha. Yeah, I'd have had him brought in. What else can ya do?"

"Oh. Something else. The Juvenile gals brought in Ingrid, too. She's still a juvenile, seventeen years old. They want to hold her until she's eighteen."

"When's she eighteen?"

Martha grimaced and shook her head. "Day after tomorrow. Can you beat that? Saturday afternoon and night, Sunday— Monday she's eighteen. So far I haven't been able to talk them out of sending her out to the detention center."

"Cap'n in?"

"Yes. He's in his office."

"Ask him to pull rank on 'em. If he hasn't got enough, ask him to call the Chief."

Piers Karlsen sat handcuffed in an interrogation room. Despondent, he looked up when Columbo came in, then quickly lowered his eyes again.

Columbo gestured to the other detective in the room to leave him alone with Karlsen. "Hiya, Karlsen. Pretty dumb to leave that thing in your car, wasn't it?"

Karlsen raised his chin. "Am I that dumb? Do I impress you as that dumb? As God is my witness, that thing was planted in my car! I swear before God that I never saw it before in my life."

"Hard case to make. Have you got a lawyer yet, Mr. Karlsen?"

Karlsen shook his head.

"Y' better get one. Unless there's somethin' you really want to tell me, I'm not gonna ask you any more questions until you talk to a lawyer."

"What are they going to do with Ingrid? They brought her in, too."

"I'm tryin' to get her released. Captain Sczciegel's working on it, too."

"I wish you would. She's gotta open the store! There's lots of film and pictures there that— Oh, God!"

NOON

Columbo stopped by the detention room where Ingrid was being held to tell her she was being released. "Your dad wants you to open the store and take care of people's pictures."

Her face was red and streaked with tears. She nodded. "You know how?"

"I can handle it. He's made me work in the shop a lot of times, 'specially since I dropped out of school. He didn't do it, Lieutenant Columbo! My father didn't do it!"

"I'm inclined to believe ya. But the evidence is too much for us just to let him go."

A few minutes later Martha confirmed that LAPD had impounded Karlsen's Chevrolet, had examined it thoroughly, and had found no marks on it to suggest it had been broken into. "There are some little scratches around the inside door handle on the driver's side, but they could have come from anything. A man's ring, for example."

They met in Captain Sczciegel's office.

"If I know you, Columbo, you're gonna tell me there's something wrong with this."

"What do *you* think, Cap'n? Out of the blue we get a call from some odd character that says Karlsen tried to sell him the Buddha. It's too easy, isn't it? Too pat."

Sczciegel nodded. "I have to react to it that way. But we'll have to let the district attorney decide where he's gonna go with the case."

"I don't like it."

"There is one thing," said Sczciegel. "At 3:12 last night we got a 911 call, from a home a couple of blocks from where Karlsen lives. Probably got nothing to do with anything. But there was a shooting on the street. Guy by the name of Ed Phillips got dead. Professional auto thief. It would look like he got caught stealing a car and the owner shot him. The car took off with screeching tires. Woman who saw it from her bedroom window says it was some kind of foreign car, looked expensive. Dark green or black. The guy was killed with three shots from a 9-mm Glock. Two in the belly, one in the chest. Not very good shooting. Nobody in the neighborhood is missing a car."

Columbo looked to Martha. "What kind of car does Mrs. Cooper-Svan drive? You notice?"

"A Jaguar. British racing green. That's a dark green."

"Who caught the case?" Columbo asked.

"Kowalski. His shift ended at eight, and he went home. Nothing doing on the case right now. I sent Crime Scene out, and they finished about eight. Most of them finished their shift with that and went home. One's left, I think. Come to think of it, she worked with you at the Svan residence. You remember Jean Pavlov?"

Columbo found Pavlov at her desk, sorting and labeling the photographs she'd taken at the scene of the street shooting.

"Hiya, Jean."

"Hey, Columbo. What brings you to the mines?"

"Coupla things. It's my day off, but I got a call to come in, 'cause we got a break in the Gunnar Svan case. That shooting you worked on this morning— There's a possibility, remote possibility, it could have somethin' to do with the Svan case. The connection isn't much: just that the guy we got in custody lives two blocks from where this other guy got shot. Our suspect claims the jade Buddha was *planted* in his car. The guy that got shot was a professional car thief, who'd know how to get into a car and plant—"

"You're way ahead of me, Columbo. What could *I* know about that possible connection?"

"Prob'ly nothin'. But Kowalski's gone home to get some sleep, and I thought you might know something odd about the case, something that might suggest—"

"There's only one thing odd about the case," said Jean Pavlov. "And it may not amount to anything. C'mon. We'll have to go to the property room."

The clerk at the counter of the property room brought out a long, thin, brown-paper package. They unwrapped it.

"There are no fingerprints on it," said Jean.

"But my, look at the engraving!"

"Embossing."

"Whatever. Artwork."

"It's a ceremonial sword of a Masonic order, the Knights Templars. I'd guess it's about a hundred years old."

Columbo frowned and ran his left hand through his hair.

"Busted off at both ends. Why would somebody—? And no fingerprints!"

"I can give you an idea what it is, Lieutenant," said the clerk behind the counter.

"Y' can?"

"Yes," she said. "We've got a lot of those on the shelves. It's a car-theft tool. Shove a blade like that between the rubber seal and the glass of a car window, and you can pry the latch handle out. On most cars. I never saw one made from an antique sword before, but it would work the same way."

"Interestin' . . . interestin'. Thank ya."

"Well, something more, Lieutenant. This is the second blade we're keeping as evidence in the Phillips shooting. There's another one, same idea. And it's got prints on it. Kowalski brought it in during the night and turned it over for a fingerprint examination. The print guys delivered it here, wrapped in plastic, which means it's got prints on it."

Columbo blinked his eyes and shook his head, as if this information mystified him. "I thank ya again. That's even more interestin'."

They returned to Jean's desk. On the way they picked up coffee.

"Say, do ya mind if I eat an egg?" Columbo asked. He pulled a hard-boiled egg from his raincoat pocket. "Like one? I got two. Wouldn't have any salt in your desk?"

She laughed. "You eat them both, Columbo. I've had my breakfast. And, yes, I do happen to have some salt." She handed him a little envelope.

"All the comforts of home," he said as he cracked the egg on the edge of her desk. "Listen. What have we got here? How far from the shooting was that blade found?"

Jean reached for her notebook. "Eighty-four feet."

"So he didn't just throw up his hands and toss it when

he was shot. He didn't try to throw it like a knife at the person who shot him, either. I mean— You couldn't throw that thing eighty-four feet."

"Maybe the person who shot him was another car thief, who wanted this car particularly."

"Or maybe this blade's got nothin' to do with anything," said Columbo. "How'd ya come to find it?"

"The paperboy saw it as he came by on his bicycle. Whatta ya want to bet it wasn't there yesterday? Anybody on the street would notice it, and it's not the kind of thing you'd just walk past and not see."

Columbo salted and munched on his egg. "Mrs. Columbo keeps a bowl of these in the fridge, so I can stick one or two in my pocket when I leave the house. Makes a nice snack. Sure you won't have the other one?"

"No, thanks. Did you get my report about the hair?"

"Uh . . . no."

"I put it on your desk."

"Sometimes I don't get around to readin' what's on my desk. I should. I really should."

Jean Pavlov smiled and shook her head. "The hair found on Gunnar Svan's car seat matches the sample you gave me. Microscopic analysis. What was on the car seat is Ingrid Karlsen's hair—some of it pubic hair."

"So Ingrid was telling the truth when she said she had sex with Svan in his car. The little devil!"

TWELVE

Columbo sat in The Store, with Mac, the detective from Vice. His day off had been spoiled. Mrs. C was playing bridge tonight. So, he figured he might as well check out something he needed to check out. Tomorrow was a day off, for sure.

His raincoat rested on the extra chair. He had left his revolver at home in the hall closet, wrapped in a bath towel as usual.

"I had a word with Cap'n Sczciegel about you, Mac. He said, put in an application for transfer to Homicide, and he'll review your record."

"Thanks, Columbo. I appreciate it."

"Get a case like the Svan case on your platter, you may decide not to thank me."

"I thought you closed that one. I heard you got a suspect in custody."

"Well . . . Not really. Y' see, in Homicide ya gotta be as much interested in not convicting the innocent as in convicting the guilty. Excuse me if I sound like a school-teacher."

"Any lessons you wanta teach me, I'll be glad to get. Hey! Like I said before, you guys are the *elite!* You guys in Homicide don't even get accused of stealin'."

"We don't get the opportunity," said Columbo with a wry smile. "Like, what could you steal off a dead person? Me, I've never been tempted. But I gotta admit, I never had temptation thrown at me much."

"*I* have," said Mac. "Y' bust in on a hooker and a john. The john's willing to hand you all the cash he's got and get you more, to be let out of it and not have his name smeared. I know guys who've taken it. I swear I never did, Columbo. I never did." He'd spoken gravely, but now he grinned. "They never have enough on 'em to make the risk worth-while. I check their IDs, maybe run that through to see if I've got a wanted guy here, then tell the guy to scram."

"Y' don't make the hookers much, either."

"Depends. If they've been muggin', if they've got a pimp that mugs— If she works quiet, doesn't offend people in the neighborhood . . . what the hell? If we do make 'em, almost every one of 'em will be out before noon the next day. Unless they flunk the health check."

"Anyway," said Columbo. "Pamela—"

"Okay. This may be a good night. See the guy at the table three away and to the right? Brush cut. Sharp nose. His name is Haddad. He's with Bunko. I don't think I should go near him. Lotsa people in here know who I am. You might go over and ID yourself."

Columbo nodded. He went to the table. "Hiya, Haddad," he said. "Columbo, Homicide. Talk a little?"

"Sure. Have a seat."

Columbo sat down. Haddad had the appearance of a prosperous businessman out for a night on the town. He wore a dark-gray suit with black pinstripes. His gray neck-tie lay neatly on his white shirt. "I've heard your name, Lieutenant. How'd you know who I am?"

"Mac over there's from Vice. I wouldn't be surprised there's guys in here from Robbery, Special Victims, and who knows what else? I couldn't tell ya who's workin' and who's here to see the show."

"Which are you here for?"

"I'm workin', and I guess you are. On the same problem. Pamela Starr."

Haddad nodded. Plainly, he did not welcome intrusion in *his* investigation.

"I'm still workin' on the Gunnar Svan murder," said Columbo.

"I know."

"Mr. Svan gave Pamela a very expensive car."

"She earned it," said Haddad dryly. "She was his pro-curess."

"The question is, what did she have to do with his death, if anything?"

"That's your line. What do you think?"

"How bad a girl is she, Haddad?"

"Not so bad. Look what she's still doing for a living: tak-ing off her clothes in a joint. She couldn't have much going for her if she's still doing that."

"Two reasons, I can think of," said Columbo. "It could be a front, to make guys like us think she's not so bad. Also, could be the way she makes her contacts."

"You figure she killed Svan and stole the jade Buddha? Or fingered him for somebody who did?"

Columbo turned up the palms of his hands and frowned. "It's a possibility I gotta look into," he said. "I doubt it. But I gotta know."

"See the guy over there?" Haddad asked, nodding toward a man two tables away.

Columbo looked at the man. He was grossly overweight, with hanging jowls and a protruding lower lip. He wore a loud jacket and fat rings. He sat with a blond, who smiled on him, fawned on him. "Jacky Di Giacomo," he muttered. "I'd recognize him anywhere. You know the story? I had him dead to rights, Haddad. When they came up with that alibi witness—"

"I know the story. Recognize the broad?"

Columbo shook his head. He'd taken her for one of the strippers who worked the stage, in her skintight pink mini-dress, conspicuous bleach job, and exaggerated makeup. She was also more than a little bit tipsy.

"You ought to. She recognizes you. So does Jacky. They've been staring at you. She's Beverly, the coy little schoolteacher who testified for Jacky at the murder trial."

"Changed her style," said Columbo wryly. "Needed rimless spectacles then."

"Wears contacts now. She lives in Aspen. Doesn't come to LA very often. When she does, she makes a point of seeing the guy who made her new life as a ski bum possible."

"They made a fool of me."

"No, Columbo. Everybody . . . *everybody* understood but the jury. That's what expensive defense lawyers are for, isn't it? To fool the jury."

"Well . . . Not much chance here, is there? Everybody knows everybody."

"They didn't know *me,* until you came over to sit with me," said Haddad.

"Oh. I spoiled your game."

"The little game. Not the big one."

"What's the big game, Haddad?"

"Not to get Pamela Starr on bunko charges. To get Di Giacomo on something important enough to settle him into San Quentin for big time."

"If he'd boosted a jade Buddha—"

"That would've been very convenient," said Haddad. "He won't make it that easy."

Pamela Starr was introduced and came onstage. She was the featured performer, the headliner. She wore a long, tight black dress glittering with sequins, black opera gloves, and spike-heeled black shoes. A feather boa was draped around her shoulders. Under the stage lights her makeup did not appear as garish as Columbo had judged it when he saw it before. In the light of spots and floods, she looked almost fresh and young.

Ten minutes after she came onstage she was stark naked. For a while she used the feather boa to tease the crowd; then she tossed that away. The lights turned redder and dimmed a little, not enough to obscure the nude figure on the stage. She danced ten minutes more. At the end, the lights came on full bright again, and Pamela Starr stood with her hands above her head, then on her hips, smiling and bowing to raucous applause.

"Interestin'," Columbo muttered to Haddad. "She's kinda interestin', isn't she?"

"Didn't you ever see her before?"

"Never saw her act before."

"A dying breed, strippers," said Haddad. "Not many of these clubs left anymore."

"Tell ya what, Haddad. I gotta get some information from somebody. May help me. May help you. I'll call ya if I find out anything."

2

Columbo walked into Karlsen's photofinishing shop. Ingrid was behind the counter, dressed in faded blue jeans and a white T-shirt. The place smelled of chemicals, and a machine was running in the back room, sloshing chemicals around and, he supposed, developing film.

"Happy birthday, Ingrid," he said. He handed her a box of doughnuts and a big paper cup of coffee.

"Sure," she said glumly, not without some hostility. "Sure. 'Happy birthday.' Big deal."

"What'd y' do yesterday?"

"Got with some kids and went to the beach. Tried to get my mind off—"

"You might wanta be nice to me, Ingrid. If it wasn't for me, you'd have spent yesterday in the juvenile detention center. They were gonna hold you until today, when you're eighteen. Coupla guys went to bat for you."

"Thanks loads," she said sarcastically.

"There's another reason you might be glad to see me, if you think about it."

"Name it."

"The fact I'm here means I'm still workin' on the murder of Gunnar Svan. Since the Buddha was found in your father's car and so on, I might've decided the case is closed."

"My father didn't kill Gunnar."

"Then why don'tcha help me find out who did?"

She shrugged. She opened the box and took out one of the half dozen doughnuts he'd brought her. "What do *I* know? I was just in love with the guy."

"Maybe you know nothin'. Maybe you know somethin' that'll be helpful."

"You have one?" she asked, pointing at the doughnuts.

"No, thanks. But I will eat an egg."

Ingrid at long last smiled, though faintly, as she watched him pull a hard-boiled egg from his raincoat pocket and crack it on the counter. He had a little envelope of salt, too, and very carefully salted the egg.

"One time," he said, "I confused the bowls of eggs in the refrigerator and got one that wasn't boiled. Cracked it like that, an'— Egg all over everything."

Ingrid laughed.

"Look," he said. "How you didn't get in juvenile trouble I'll never know, but you didn't, and that's all in the past now. Let me confirm somethin' that you told me. You had sex with Gunnar Svan late in the afternoon of the day he died, in his car, out in the hills. Right?"

"Right."

"About what time was that?"

"Uh . . . When he dropped me off at home it was a quarter to six."

"You'd testify to that in court if you were asked?"

"Right."

"Those strands of hair you gave me matched ones found on the front seat of his car."

"Surprised?"

"No. But it's important. Now, somethin' else. I need to know exactly how you came to meet Gunnar Svan. How'd you come to be let in when you went over to Arizona and showed up where he was shooting a picture?"

Ingrid drew a deep breath. "Well . . . I was introduced to him."

"I imagine you were at that. By who?"

"Pam. Actually, she didn't introduce me. She sent me to

Arizona. She said it'd be okay, he'd see me. She told me to go to the place where they were shooting and ask for a guy named Ron. I did. Ron was expecting me."

"*Why* did you go see Gunnar Svan?"

"I wanted to get in the movies. Pam said he'd help me. I wasn't dumb, though. I knew he'd expect something." She smiled. "He actually went through an act, a charade I guess you'd call it, of having me read for him. Of course, it had to be . . . in the nude."

"So what happened?"

"I'm not dumb. By the time I'd been with him a couple of days, the guy was really hot for me! Hey, if he hadn't got killed—"

"If he hadn't got killed, somebody might have blackmailed him, 'cause you were a juvenile. What do you think of *that* possibility?"

"Pam?"

"Maybe not. She wasn't in a very good position. She'd corrupted a juvenile herself."

" 'Corrupted . . .' "

"Yeah, corrupted. Besides sending you to Arizona, she came over there and took part in a threesome. You don't have to deny it. She told me. How'd you meet Pam?"

"A man introduced me."

"Who?"

"Mr. Di Giacomo."

"How'd ya meet *him?*"

"Bunch of us. The guys had bikes."

"Motorcycles."

"Sure. Anyway, we were in the parking lot at a McDonald's, and Mr. Di Giacomo came over to our bunch. Hey, Columbo!" Ingrid grinned. "Some of us were pretty good-lookin' chicks. So he asks if any of us girls are interested in getting in the movies. Sure we were. Who isn't?"

"So you gave him your name and phone number."

"Right. And next day Pam calls."

Columbo grimaced. "I don't know if I wanta know what the conversation was."

Ingrid shrugged. "Whatta ya figure?"

"Were you the only one of your friends who gave Di Giacomo a name and phone number?"

"One other girl did. We knew what he was doin'. We're not a bunch of dummies."

"That other girl. How'd it work out for her?"

"She got two grand and a mess of lumps."

"What's her name?"

"Trish Miller."

"How'd you manage to rent a car and keep it for two weeks?"

"Somebody else paid."

"Who?"

"Mr. Di Giacomo."

12:03 P.M.

It was tempting not to bow to Mrs. Yasukawa as she did to him. Instead, Columbo smiled and said he was glad to see her and hoped she was well.

"Altogether well, Lieutenant Columbo," said the pretty Japanese housemaid who worked for Mrs. Cooper-Svan. "May I serve you coffee?"

"I wish I could stay to take coffee with you, Mrs. Yasukawa, but I gotta be movin'. I just wanted to ask you to look at a picture, ask you if you ever saw the man in the picture."

Mrs. Yasukawa nodded. "Ah?"

He handed her a mug shot of Jacky Di Giacomo. "That's the man as he was four years ago. But do you think you ever saw that man?"

"Oh, yes, Sir. Yes, Sir. This man called from time to time to visit with Mr. Svan."

"Do you have any idea why?"

She shook her head. "No, Sir. It is not proper for a house-maid to try to know who her family's visitors are or why they visit."

4

1:08 P.M.

He met Martha Zimmer beside a hotdog cart on Pershing Square. If Burt sold the best chili in LA, this guy sold the best hotdogs. Columbo was an authority on that.

"So far, I can't lay anything on Muriel Paul," she said. "From all I can gather, she's just the classic good-hearted hooker."

" 'Never on Sunday,' " said Columbo.

"From all I can tell."

"Well . . . even so, she was in the house and saw the Buddha."

"Yeah, but Karlsen had the Buddha in his car! He tried to sell it."

"Right. And somebody calls and tells us to go get him." Columbo shook his head. "Isn't that *neat?*"

"You don't think he did it," she said soberly.

"Martha, I *know* he didn't do it. Question is, how'm I gonna make the DA see he didn't?"

Martha chewed on a big bite from her hotdog. She didn't agree that Burt sold the best chili, but she did agree that this guy had the best hotdogs.

"Martha. Could we make a connection between Muriel Paul and Jacky Di Giacomo?"

"If we use our imagination," she said. "I know why you'd like to—"

"He pimped Ingrid Karlsen. She'll testify he did. Underage. He visited the Cooper-Svan house and almost certainly saw the Buddha. The maid will testify he came there. He'd know how to jimmy a car door and plant somethin' in somebody else's car."

"Leaves one question open, Columbo."

"Which is?"

"Why'd a guy who'd boosted a million-dollar antique leave it in somebody else's car?"

Columbo sighed and shook his head. "Not because he saw the long arm of the law about to grab him. I'm no closer to this thing than I was—"

"You got an instinct for it, Columbo. You know who killed Svan. You'd like to find it was somebody else. It would be great if you could make a case against Di Giacomo."

5

4:02 P.M.

He walked through headquarters in his shirtsleeves, so everybody could see he was carrying his revolver. He hoped nobody asked him to take it out and show them.

He'd unloaded it and this morning had forgotten to carry the little leather case of cartridges.

Sergeant Paul Haddad was at his desk in Bunko. Also in his shirtsleeves—a crisply starched, well-pressed white shirt—his Beretta hung in his left armpit as if it had grown there when he was a child. His desk was dismayingly neat. All he had on it were a few file folders carefully stacked, edges parallel to the edges of the desktop.

"Hiya, Haddad. Got somethin' for ya."

Haddad listened studiously as Columbo told him what he'd learned about Di Giacomo and girls.

"Juvenile and Special Victims," he said. Special Victims was the new euphemism for sex crimes.

"Let's don't get hung up on jurisdiction lines, Haddad. Let's let it be your collar. I got the two names for ya: Ingrid and her friend Trish Miller. Two juveniles. With a little checking you can find others, I bet. Hey! There's blackmail in it. I'd *love* to chase it, but I've got the Svan case to close. Build it, man! You're a smart cop. Build a case Di Giacomo can't beat the way he beat my murder rap."

"I appreciate this, Lieutenant."

Columbo nodded. "Gonna ask you to do me a favor. Don't collar Di Giacomo till I get the Svan case down. You'll need a little time, anyway. Besides, it's not one hundred percent out of the question that Jacky Di Giacomo killed Svan."

6

6:22 P.M.

"We gotta quit meetin' this way, Adrienne."

They were at La Sonrisa, in one of the private booths

that faced the windows. Ai-ling Cooper-Svan's favorite watering hole. Adrienne had looked around to be sure Ai-ling was not in the place before she met Columbo there. She wouldn't mind encountering Ai-ling but didn't want to meet her unexpectedly.

She laughed. "There's no way a girl could meet *you* on the q.t., Columbo. You walk into a place like this in that flapping raincoat you won't check— My dear friend, everybody knows you're here."

"Or knows you're meeting somebody that doesn't belong here."

"Belong? *Columbo!*"

"Place like this is a little too sophisticated for me."

"Cut the crap, Columbo."

"I'm more the hotdogs and beer kind of guy."

" 'Sophisticated,' " she repeated. "Let me ask you something. If you were my boyfriend and saw the pictures of me that are going to run in *Glitz* next month, would you figure you ought to cut off the relationship?"

"No. No way. I mean, I'm not sure I'd want Mrs. Columbo to— But that's different. You're an elegant young woman. Y' know, when Mrs. C and I were the age to do that kind of thing, it just wasn't done. Nowadays . . ." He shrugged.

"Well, Dan isn't sure it won't damage his career as an architect to be identified with me."

"Aww—"

"Right. Hell with him. Listen, Columbo, I got something more important to talk about. I think Ai-ling's got the idea that you suspect *she* killed Gunnar."

"Ah, well. I don't *know* who killed Gunnar yet."

"Columbo . . . It *couldn't* have been Ai-ling. You and I have been friends a long time. You know I've got instincts about things like this." She shook her head. "It *couldn't* have been Ai-ling! She's gone through hell, Columbo. I'd like to be able to tell her you don't suspect her."

Columbo tipped his head and blew a sigh. "I'd like to be able to tell her that myself. But, y' know, so long as we don't have the murderer in custody, we can't eliminate the wife as a suspect."

"Columbo, you've *got* a man in custody."

"You're good about journalistic ethics, aren't you, Adrienne?"

"You know I am. Have something to tell me?"

"I trust you. Piers Karlsen didn't kill Gunnar Svan."

"Then who did?"

"That's what I've gotta find out."

THIRTEEN

"The DA is waiting for word on what to do about Piers Karlsen," said Captain Sczciegel. "I know you don't like the case. I don't like it either. But—"

"Let 'im go back to his shop and develop film," said Columbo. "He didn't kill Gunnar Svan."

"You're stickin' your neck out, Columbo. Way, way out. And you're stickin' mine out, too. Hell, you're stickin' the Department's neck out."

Columbo nodded. "Sometimes you just got a *feelin'* for somethin'."

"You've been thinking about it. I bet you lost sleep over it, didn't you? You look like a man who didn't get a good night's sleep."

"Actually, this morning what I've been thinkin' about is something else entirely. Cap'n . . . there's a *limerick*— You like limericks?"

"Like any man," said Captain Sczciegel. "I'm not obsessed with them."

"I sort of am. Listen. Listen to this one. It's the one that kept me awake, 'cause I couldn't think of the last line—

> "There was a young man from Duluth
> Who went out with a plumber named Ruth.
> She was good with a wrench
> But was still quite a wench—

"And where's it go from there, Cap'n? What's the last line?"

Sczciegel covered his eyes with his hands and shook his head. " 'And wrenched him in, to tell you the truth.' Something like that. Right?"

Columbo laughed. "Hey! You got it. That's what caused me to lose sleep."

"Nothing about the Svan case?"

"Yeah, somethin'. Why was everything in the basement dusty but the star drill? Little detail that keeps me awake." He nodded. "Yeah. And there's somethin' else, too. I won't mention that one just yet. It'll keep *you* awake."

"Sleep tight tonight on this one, Columbo—

> "I once knew a cutie named Judy
> That everyone said was a beauty.
> She worked on the street
> Long hours on her feet,
> So gladly lay down to do duty."

Columbo chortled. "I'll write that one down, Cap'n, so I won't forget it."

"No, you won't. I bet anything you want to bet that you've lost your pencil. Anyway, I see you're carrying your sidearm. Is it loaded?"

"Well . . . the little case of bullets is in the car."

Captain Sczciegel closed his eyes. "Columbo . . ."

2

The offices of Balzac, Tremaine & Fisher, CPAs, were in one of those buildings Columbo was glad he did not work in: square, mostly glass, modern marvels of cold efficiency.

The receptionist was colder yet, until he showed his identification as a homicide detective, Los Angeles Police Department.

"Mr. Fisher is expecting you, Lieutenant. Will you have some coffee?"

"Why, yes. I'd like some coffee. I bet ya make better coffee here than what we get at headquarters. Y' know? Instant, I can't stand. Decaf— Gimme a break!"

"Coffee with caffeine," she said.

"Yes, Ma'am. Since you offer coffee. I mean, I assume it's all made. I don't want to put you to any trouble."

She smiled. "It's all made, Lieutenant."

Frederick Fisher's officer was more interesting than the building and reception area. Fisher, it seemed, loved aquariums and tropical fish. Eight large glass tanks. Three of them appeared to be saltwater tanks, and five freshwater. In any case, the room was alive with the movement of the colorful creatures that lived in the tanks.

Fisher himself seemed like a man who would be reluctant to stick his finger in a tank, for fear of being bitten. He was cordial, shook hands, asked if Columbo had been offered coffee, and suggested they sit on a couch facing a coffee table, rather than across his desk.

"What can I do for you, Lieutenant?"

"I understand you are the accountant for Mrs. Ai-ling Cooper-Svan."

"I am. Yes, I am."

"Wonderful woman, don't ya think? Charming—"

"Yes. Absolutely. A lovely woman."

"Shrewd businesswoman, though?" Columbo asked.

"I believe I'd say that of her, Lieutenant. Yes, I would. She inherited a lot of money. Her father—off the record—is a wastrel, dissipating what he inherited at such a rate that— Well . . . He is not an admirable manager of assets, though an engaging fellow with myriad friends."

"I don't need to know, but I wonder, do they have a good relationship?"

"Mrs. Cooper-Svan and her father? Uh . . . Arm's length, Lieutenant. He wants to deny the Chinese element of their ancestry. She glories in it. But—"

"Right."

Both men paused while the receptionist arrived with a silver tray: coffee, milk, sugar, and a small plate of miniature Danish pastries.

"Mr. Fisher, the point I have to raise is, was Mr. Svan what you'd call an admirable manager of assets?"

Fisher hesitated. "I'm not sure I can talk about it, Lieutenant."

"Mr. Fisher . . . I don't want to put any pressure on you, or anything like that, but you know I'm entitled to ask. Since Mr. Svan is dead— Also, isn't it possible there was embezzlement here? If so, we've got a crime involved, and confidentiality goes out the door."

"Not entirely. I can talk about Svan, not about Mrs. Cooper-Svan."

"Good enough. Was Mr. Svan an admirable manager of assets?"

Fisher picked up a cup of coffee and a little Danish.

"Lieutenant Columbo," he said before he took a nibble or a sip, "Gunnar Svan was a *thief!* He stole from everyone he did business with. He took kickbacks. He cooked his books. I'm not going to go so far as to say I'm glad he's dead. I don't think I could say that about anyone. But he was a *bad* man, a miscreant, a liar and a cheat."

Columbo drank some coffee. "That about covers the waterfront, doesn't it, Mr. Fisher?"

"Sorry. I— To be perfectly frank, I heartily disliked the man."

"Let me ask ya a question, Sir. Am I wrong in guessing you are one of the many men who admires Mrs. Cooper-Svan—maybe more than just a little?"

Fisher put down his coffee cup. "I'm a married man, Lieutenant—with children."

"So am I. And old enough to be her father. But a man might feel protective of her, just the same."

"What does that mean, Lieutenant? What does she need to be protected from?"

"Oh, I was just thinkin' of the question of whether or not Mr. Svan had been stealing from Mrs. Cooper-Svan."

Fisher glanced around the room, sighed, frowned. "I shouldn't talk about it. But . . . Yes, he was stealing from her! And not just a little, either. He was stealing from others, but from her more than anyone else."

"Did she know it?"

Fisher nodded. "I'm saying more than I should."

"Okay. If he was stealing money, what was he doing with it? Where is it now?"

"A damned good question," said Fisher grimly.

"He didn't spend it all, did he? I mean, even if he *did* buy Pamela Starr a BMW—"

"It's hard to trace," said Fisher. "Transactions were in cash."

"Maybe the Internal Revenue Service can trace them," Columbo suggested.

"They're trying. They've come up with a name." Fisher turned and pulled a file from a drawer in his credenza. He opened it and flipped pages. "Wallenstein. Eric Wallenstein. Limelight Electric paid a kickback to Svan. They were instructed to deliver the money in cash to Eric Wallenstein. He's a onetime mutual fund broker, suspended from trading by the SEC."

"What was the relationship between Wallenstein and Svan?" Columbo asked.

Fisher smiled wanly. "That's what everybody wants to know."

"Does Mrs. Cooper-Svan know about this?"

"No. The IRS only came up with it the week before the murder. I haven't bothered her with it."

"Nobody's come across the name Jacky Di Giacomo?"

"No. I don't think I've ever heard that name."

11:04 A.M.

Ai-ling sat in her office, scowling at the television set. Link had called her to tell her about a news story he had heard on the radio. Now she watched it. It was true.

The announcer intoned the item— "Piers Karlsen, held since Saturday on suspicion he was responsible for the murder of film director Gunnar Svan, has been released on posting $10,000 bond. The office of the district attorney said that, while Karlsen remains a suspect in the case, the evidence against him is incomplete and that holding him would probably ruin his small business. Mr. Karlsen owns a photofinishing shop. While free on bond, Mr. Karlsen will wear a beeper radio on his ankle, which will keep the police reliably informed of his whereabouts at all times."

The station had no tape of Karlsen. The picture switched to the shop and to a picture of Ingrid.

"Karlsen's eighteen-year-old daughter Ingrid has been running the family business as best she can while her father was in the county jail. Miss Karlsen, tell us— Did your father kill Gunnar Svan?"

Ingrid stared into the camera and shook her head firmly. "No way. In the first place, my father would never kill anybody. He's not that kind of person. Besides, Mr. Svan was a friend of the family."

"There is a story around that you spent some time with him on a movie set in Arizona."

"Yes. He was very kind. He showed me all about how pictures are made. I, uh—" She smiled at the camera. "—am interested in being in pictures, like any girl, and he let me watch them shoot and explained exactly what was going on. He was a real friend—of my father's, too."

Ai-ling switched off the television set. *"Goddamn!"* she muttered.

4

11:31 A.M.

Ai-ling picked up her telephone.

"Lieutenant Columbo is on line two, Mrs. Cooper-Svan. Do you want to talk to him?"

"I suppose I better." She punched in the line-two key. "Good morning, Columbo. What can I do for you?"

"Have you heard we let Mr. Karlsen go on bail this morning?"

"Yes. I must say I'm a little surprised, considering the tape and the Buddha."

"Well, I'll hafta explain it to ya sometime. The way we figure, the man's gonna lose his business, his livelihood. Besides, he's wearing one of those signaler gimmicks that tells us where he is all the time."

"Are you pursuing some other lead, Lieutenant?"

"As a matter of fact, yes, Ma'am. It seems Mr. Svan had some odd friends. Anyway, I called to say you can pick up your Buddha anytime. I'd bring it to ya, but I wouldn't feel right, carrying a million-dollar antique in my car. Strange thing— There are no fingerprints on the Buddha. It's been wiped clean."

"That's what the thief would do, wouldn't he, Lieutenant?"

"Well, maybe. On the other hand, we didn't find any strange fingerprints anywhere in the house. If the murderer was smart, he wore gloves, probably rubber gloves. I bet he never touched the jade without gloves. So why would he wipe off other people's fingerprints? Yours and Mr. Svan's were to be expected. And I've had suggestions that there might have been one or two other sets."

"Whose?"

"People whose names you know. Pamela Murphy and Muriel Paul. You know they were in your house. Pamela Murphy told me Mr. Svan let her handle the Buddha."

"He let her sleep in my bed," Ai-ling said resentfully.

"Yeah. Well, it does seem odd that the fingerprints were all wiped off."

"Maybe the murderer-burglar was an amateur."

"Right. Anyway, as I say, you can pick up your property anytime. So I won't bother ya anymore right now."

"No bother, Lieutenant. Call whenever I can be of help."

"Well— Oh say, there is one other thing. A man came to your house to visit Mr. Svan. His name's Di Giacomo. Ever hear of him?"

"No, never."

"And one more name, if ya don't mind. Eric Wallenstein."

"My husband thought of Wallenstein as a sort of business adviser. A creepy character, in my judgment."

"Thank ya, Mrs. Cooper-Svan. I'll let you know if anything breaks."

5

12:42 P.M.

"For nothing! For goddamned nothing! The risk and—"

Ai-ling stopped. Link did not know she had killed a man Saturday morning, and she was not going to tell him. The story had run small in the newspapers. The man had been called Ed Phillips, and he was a professional auto thief, as she had guessed. He had served time. As she had also guessed, he had been high on crack cocaine.

Even so— She would never forget his puzzled question, asked as if he could not understand the situation at all— "Sis . . . Why you want hurt Ed? You *kill* Ed!"

Yes, she had hurt Ed, and killed him. In self-defense.

"That damned Columbo is focusing on me!"

Link glanced around, concerned that she might be heard. They had met in a restaurant where she could not smoke, and that was not good for her composure. "Maybe we should go to the bar," he suggested. "Where you can smoke."

She ignored him. "I've got the damned Buddha back. I need it like I need a hole in the head."

"Think, Ai-ling. Think! What could Lieutenant Columbo possibly have against you? They had a whole lot more on Karlsen, and he's out on bail."

"That's the whole damned point! Planting the Buddha didn't do a bit of good."

"My suggestion is that we leave the thing alone," said Link. "Let Lieutenant Columbo try to make his case. You said you'd outsmart a detective like him. So far, you have."

"A chip of glass out in the yard. That's all he has, isn't it? He can't build a case on that. The murderer could have accidentally kicked it out."

"Exactly. He can't build a case on that."

"Even so . . . I'm going to retain a lawyer."

1:18 P.M.

Adrienne had agreed to meet Columbo if this time it did not have to be at Burt's, or beside a hotdog cart. A modest restaurant, then, he had said, where he could get something simple. They sat over plates of fish and chips.

"You've worked this town for some time," he said to her. "I imagine you know the story of Jacky Di Giacomo."

"Sure."

"He arranged Ingrid Karlsen's visit to Arizona."

"If you can prove that, you have him after all."

"That'd be nice, but it doesn't tell me who killed Gunnar Svan. What do you know about a guy called Eric Wallenstein?"

"Small-timer. Lost his securities license. He's been involved in a lot of things."

"Like maybe stealing Mrs. Cooper-Svan blind."

"Like really?"

"Really. What can y' tell me about him?"

Adrienne rubbed her hands together for a moment, as she thought. "Okay. Wallenstein came to LA from New Jersey, ten years ago or like that. He sold mutual funds. After he sold highly questionable, or worthless, mutual funds to a number of elderly people and bilked them out of their retirement savings, the SEC took away his license to sell. People sued him. He wrung himself out in bankruptcy. Since then he's been around town, always involved in something shady."

"A contractor who paid a kickback to Svan was told to pay it in cash to Wallenstein."

"Money laundering," said Adrienne. "Tax evasion."

"Mrs. Cooper-Svan says her husband used Wallenstein as a financial adviser."

"Okay, Columbo, answer me something. What's the point? What're you after?"

"You told me you got an instinct that Mrs. Cooper-Svan didn't kill her husband. I'd like to think that's right. So— Gunnar Svan was associating with some shady characters. One of them could have planted the Buddha in Karlsen's car. I got an instinct that Karlsen is not the murderer. You got one that Mrs. C-S isn't. So?"

"Be careful, Columbo," Adrienne said soberly. "The story of how Di Giacomo got away with murder is pretty well known. Some lawyer is gonna say you went on a vendetta against him."

Columbo shrugged. "I'm an honest cop."

"I know that. But you could be sticking your neck out."

He raised his eyebrows, tipped his head, and turned down the corners of his mouth. "Part of the game, Adrienne. Just part of the game."

3:02 P.M.

When they left the restaurant the Peugeot wouldn't start. Columbo called AAA, and forty-five minutes later a service truck arrived.

"Dead battery," said the mechanic. "I'll boost it."

"Huh-uh," said Columbo. He pulled the butt of a cigar from his mouth. "Believe me, I've been through this before. See that gizmo right there? What d' ya call that? Just put a wrench on that and turn it a quarter of a turn to the right."

"Mister, this battery is *dead!*"

Adrienne laughed. "Better listen to him, fellow," she said to the mechanic. "In his pocket he's carrying a badge, and in his armpit he's got a pistol."

"Huh? Huh? So?" the mechanic said, waving his arms. "You gonna shoot me for telling you your battery's dead?"

Columbo shook his head and fluttered his hands. "Never mind all that. Ya see, my car's a *French* car. I don't know how it works. But it works different from American cars and Japanese cars. Try it my way once, will ya? Just turn that gadget a quarter of a turn to the right, and—"

"Mister, if that's the way it works, why didn't *you* turn it?"

" 'Cause, you're the one with *tools*. That's why I called ya: to bring your tools."

The mechanic glanced at Adrienne, who leaned on the fender of the Peugeot and laughed with tears running down her cheeks. "Lady. You think I should do it his way?"

"Do it his way! You're in the presence of a certifiable genius."

The mechanic shook his head scornfully, but he put a metric wrench on Columbo's "gizmo" and turned it a quarter turn clockwise.

" 'Kay. Right. Now, lessee."

Columbo scrambled in behind the wheel, turned on the ignition, and pressed the starter. The old engine surged to life.

Columbo looked up, grinned and shrugged, and said, "Y' see. This car's a *French* car. It's different."

FOURTEEN

1

WEDNESDAY, AUGUST 12—10:21 A.M.

Columbo and an officer from Juvenile Division drove to Malibu Beach. Miss Cabot—Columbo didn't know her first name or even her title—was a severe-looking blond, who made it plain by her tone and manner that she took no nonsense and expected complete cooperation from everyone she dealt with—maybe even from Columbo.

She had called him and asked if he wanted to go to Malibu with her. He'd given her the tip on the case, and she knew he was interested in it—interested beyond the fact that a child had been corrupted and abused.

Miss Cabot had gone to see Trish Miller's mother earlier that morning, where the mother worked as a waitress in a diner. The mother had said her daughter could almost certainly be found on the beach at Malibu and probably could be found by looking for the white '91 Ford Probe her boyfriend drove. Trish had bought a bright-red bikini on Monday and would be wearing it today. Mrs. Miller also showed Miss Cabot a billfold photograph of her daughter.

How old was Trish? Sixteen, not quite seventeen.

Columbo had said there was no point in taking two cars to Malibu and he'd be glad to drive. When they reached his car in the garage, Miss Cabot had all but refused to get in.

"Y' see, it's a French car," Columbo explained.

"Undercover?"

"I guess y' could say that."

"Well . . . In that case—"

When they were on the Santa Monica Freeway, she shook her head and said, "Lieutenant, there's no radio in this car!"

"Right. I figure havin' a radio in a car is like havin' a phone; somebody can always get ya and interrupt what you're doin'. I stop and call in once in a while."

"I thought regulations *required* a two-way radio in every police vehicle."

"Right. But this is *my* car. It doesn't belong to the Department."

Miss Cabot shook her head again. "We're supposed to drive— Okay. Never mind."

He cruised along the parking at Malibu until he came to a white Ford Probe. He parked—illegally but showing police identification on his dashboard—and he and Miss Cabot walked out on the beach.

In the open air, with wind blowing, Columbo lit a cigar.

"Bright-red bikini," said Cabot. They walked up to a knot of teenagers. "Trish Miller?" she asked.

A thin, pallid boy stood. "Who wants to know?" he challenged.

"The fuzz," said Miss Cabot. "Buzz off, sonny boy."

"By what authority?"

"By authority of a run downtown. And a stay until your parents come to get you. Make fifty yards, smart-ass. And don't come closer till you get *specific* permission."

The boy backed off. The others got up and edged away.

Miss Cabot spoke to the girl in the red bikini. "The way we hear it, you got two thousand dollars and lumps."

The girl stood. Her eyes were wide, her face flushed. "Me?"

"You. Let me introduce Lieutenant Columbo, LAPD Homicide. He's interested in your two thousand dollars and lumps."

The girl gasped. *"Homicide?"*

Miss Cabot nodded. "How's that awful, awful old cliché have it? 'You are known by the company you keep.' Ahh, Trish, Trish. Let's sit down in the sand and talk about the company you've kept."

The girl rubbed tears from her eyes. "I didn't—"

"Figure you prob'ly didn't," said Columbo. He met Miss Cabot's eyes. They'd play white-hat–black-hat, okay? She understood.

Trish Miller was not just a beautiful girl; she was extraordinarily beautiful: petite yet full-figured, with an exquisite little face and soft, light-brown hair. That she liked herself was obvious. She had reason. But right now she was afraid.

"Why'd somebody pay you two thousand dollars, Trish?" asked Miss Cabot.

"Who says somebody did?"

"Never mind who says. Somebody did. We know that much. And you got smacked around. You know why, and you know what kind of trouble you're in. You want to help yourself, or do we just take it down the line?"

"Hey, guys! What's Homicide got to do with anything?" the girl asked.

"Put it another way, Miss," said Columbo. He drew on

his cigar. "What've you got to do with homicide? Answer: probl'y nothin'. We're not talkin' of makin' you on a homicide charge. Okay? But . . . you may know stuff that's got to do with homicide."

"In which case, you've got a big chance to help yourself out," said Miss Cabot.

The teenagers stood away at a respectful distance and stared as their friend was—as they saw it—harassed.

"Whatta you want to know?"

"Why did somebody pay you two thousand dollars?" asked Miss Cabot.

Trish Miller glanced toward the staring friends. "To shut me up," she said. "So I wouldn't go to the cops about what happened."

"What happened?"

"A guy beat up on me."

"What guy?" asked Miss Cabot. "Where? When? Why? The whole story."

The girl sighed. "It happened at the Sunset Motel in Bel Air. I was supposed to give this guy you-know-what. As soon as I saw him, I didn't want to. He was a *giant!* I mean, he was one of the biggest men I ever saw, with muscles— I guess I must have looked scared, and it made him mad. He was drunk, and he got wild. He punched me in the face and in the stomach, and then he threw me down and kicked me. I screamed. Guys busted in. There was a hell of a scene. Then a man came in and gave everybody money to quiet down. And he took me to his car, then to his apartment, and took care of me the rest of the night. And he gave me two thousand dollars."

"Who was this man who gave you the two thousand dollars?"

"Mr. Di Giacomo."

"Who was the man who beat you?"

"I don't know. Nobody mentioned his name."

"When did this happen?"

"It was the night of the Fourth of July."

Columbo sat puffing on his cigar, listening, and let Miss Cabot ask the questions.

"How did you get to be at this motel and in this room with this man?"

"Mr. Di Giacomo arranged it. I was sort of . . . working for him."

"Working— Sure. Turning tricks, hmm?" said Miss Cabot grimly.

Trish nodded.

"Was Ingrid doing the same thing?" Columbo asked. "Had Mr. Di Giacomo turned her into a—"

"Not really. Ingrid had a different deal. With her there was just one guy. I guess you know all about it; you're the guy in charge of the investigation of the murder of Gunnar Svan. I recognize you."

Miss Cabot picked up the questioning again. "Ingrid just had one guy, you say. How many did you take care of?"

"Four. After what happened, Mr. Di Giacomo wouldn't let me work for him anymore."

"How much did you get paid each time?"

"Fifty dollars."

Miss Cabot shook her head. "Sixteen years old. Sixteen years old and turning tricks. I should take you in, Trish. I really should. What'd you do with the two thousand?"

"I gave it to my mother, for the same reason Mr. Di Giacomo gave it to me, to quiet her down. She put it in the bank. Oh, yeah. I've got a bankbook that shows it's there, but I can't take it out."

"Where's your father?"

Trish shrugged and turned down the corners of her mouth. "Where's who?"

"I'm going to keep an eye on you, young lady. You'll have to come and see me every two weeks, and I'll be checking on you now and then. Is the mouthy creep your boyfriend?"

The girl nodded.

"How old is he?"

"Eighteen."

"You tell him I expect you to be home by midnight every night. If he keeps you out later, *he'll* be in trouble."

Trish looked toward the boy, then lowered her eyes.

"Lieutenant—" said Miss Cabot.

Columbo pulled his cigar from his mouth. "I guess I've heard it all. Yeah. With this, I really have heard it all." He stood and swatted the sand off the tail of his raincoat.

"Okay, Trish," said Miss Cabot. "Here's my card. I'm writing on the back. Wednesday, August nineteenth, two o'clock. You be at my office."

The girl took the card. She stared at it for a moment, then tucked it into the bra of her bikini.

Columbo was already on his way up the beach. But he stopped. "Oh, say, Miss Miller, I do want to ask you one little thing. Uh— You say Ingrid's deal was different. What kind of different?"

"All kinds of different. I mean, she drove Gunnar's car sometimes. She had a key to his house. The deal didn't last very long, but while it did— Hey, she had a key to his house! When she knew his wife was out of town, she'd go over there with a couple of kids and swim in his pool, drink his liquor—"

11:02 A.M.

Ai-ling sat at her desk, looking over the layout for the article on Adrienne Boswell. She had assigned the writing to her best writer, and he had done a good job—though she had fed him most of the text. He had interviewed Adrienne only once and had relied more on what Ai-ling told him.

Anyway, it was not the text that was going to sell the October issue of *Glitz*. Los Angeles would be fascinated by photographs of the tall, handsome, red-haired journalist in the nude. Of an actress or wannabe actress this sort of thing was expected, but nude pictures of a woman who had distinguished herself in a profession where exhibitionism was forbidden would be a sensation.

Already Ai-ling had begun to look for others. She had spoken on the phone with a lawyer in the district attorney's office, but the woman had said she was afraid she'd lose her job if she posed nude. Link had spoken with a fellow psychiatrist, and she had not said no; she'd said she would think about it.

Out of some sense of what they must have thought was propriety, the workmen had stayed away from the house and not finished pounding holes in the basement floor. But they had finished now. They had taken away all their tools. The star drill was gone. And Lieutenant Columbo, smart though he was, had not identified it as the weapon used to bash in Gunnar's skull.

So what did he have? What could he possibly have except that a shard of glass had fallen outside? Nothing.

Probably she had panicked in stashing the Buddha in Karlsen's Chevrolet.

Anyway, now she had the Buddha back. It sat on the credenza behind her. It was worth a million dollars, and whenever she left the office she locked it in a heavy safe set in the wall behind a print.

She turned her attention again to the Adrienne Boswell layout. In a few more days they would close the October issue. It had to be in print in two more weeks, so it could go on sale in September.

NOON

Captain Sczciegel had called a conference on the Gunnar Svan murder. They sat around a conference table, munching on boxed lunches and sipping from cans of soda. The captain, Columbo, Martha Zimmer, Paul Haddad, and a man from the office of the district attorney: Hal Berwyn.

"Columbo," the captain said, "we don't mean to put pressure on you, but the man will have been dead two weeks tomorrow, and—"

"It's not too easy, Cap'n. I've told you. I got a pretty good idea who did it, but I'd like to have more evidence before I lay it all out."

"Explain to us, Lieutenant Columbo," said Hal Berwyn, "why you reject Piers Karlsen as a suspect."

Berwyn was a diminutive man, very precise in his features and in his speech. He had ordered a salad, not a sandwich, for his box lunch.

"Mr. Berwyn— What evidence we got?"

"You are not impressed with the Buddha, with finding the million-dollar Buddha in his car?"

"Sir— If you'd stolen a million-dollar antique, would *you* leave it in your car?"

"Gotta remember something, Columbo," said Captain Sczciegel. "How many times do we find killers still in possession of the murder weapon when we come to nab them? Guys who kill other people don't think straight."

"Okay," said Columbo. "So we get this call from a guy who won't say who he is. 'Hey, I can tell ya where the million-dollar Buddha is.' Isn't that odd? Am I the only one who thinks that's curious?"

"Alright," said Berwyn in a tone of labored patience. "What about his threatening, on the tape Mrs. Cooper-Svan gave us?"

"Odd tape, that," said Columbo. "How's it come that it starts just when Karlsen starts to talk tough and ends just when he threatens to take care of the matter 'some other way'? It's got a neat beginning and ending, hasn't it?"

"You know what this implies," said Berwyn darkly.

"Yes, Sir. And I hope it's not true. I got another idea about the case. I hope *it* turns out to be the answer."

After the meeting, Captain Sczciegel asked Columbo to step aside with him for a moment. "Hey," he said. "Don't get too deep into the Jacky Di Giacomo business. You know what I mean. It could look like you got a vendetta going against that guy. It could look like the LAPD got a vendetta on against him."

"Understood, Cap'n."

4

2:11 P.M.

Ingrid was behind the counter at her father's shop. He was in the rear, in a darkroom. Columbo wondered if having Ingrid, in her tight, skimpy blue-denim shorts, behind the counter didn't improve the business.

"You didn't tell me somethin', little girl."

"What?"

"You didn't tell me you had a key to the Svan house."

"You didn't ask."

"What became of that key?"

She filled with breath and sighed. "I gave it to Mr. Di Giacomo."

"When?"

"Two days before—"

"Why?"

"He asked for it."

5

8:05 P.M.

Jacky Di Giacomo sat down beside Eric Wallenstein in The Store. Wallenstein had chosen a booth in the back of the room, where they would not be noticed. Everyone else wanted to sit near the stage.

A cute little blond was strutting around naked on the stage. This was Amateur Night, and she was supposed to be a secretary having a glorious night doing something she had always dreamed of doing. In fact, she stripped every other night of the week in a club in Long Beach.

"I want a straight answer to a straight question," Wallenstein said to Di Giacomo.

Di Giacomo didn't like to be challenged, and he scowled. He didn't frighten Wallenstein, who was a husky, broad-shouldered man, in shape to give Di Giacomo a shot in the gut with a hammy fist any time he wanted to. He was not, though, the kind of man who would shoot a hammy fist. He was a smooth, suave man, a confidence man of the first rank: a salesman, a persuader.

"What's your straight question?"

"I want to know, straight out, no messing around, if you killed Gunnar Svan."

"If I killed Svan, I'd have the Buddha," muttered Di Giacomo. "It's worth more than—"

"Except one thing."

"What?"

"His silence."

Di Giacomo snorted. " 'His silence,' " he scoffed.

"You screwed the deal, Mister. We were picking up a lot of loose change. Then you decided to play to the man's gross tastes, for more money."

"*I* decided? It's how I kept him on the reservation. Hey! What if the guy'd spilled to the IRS?"

"Who killed him, Di Giacomo?"

"How th' hell do I know? I promise you, as God is my witness, I didn't have nothin' to do with it!"

"God is your witness. Give me a better witness."

"Hey . . . I had ideas about the Buddha. But I wouldn't have had to kill him to get it. I had a key to his house."

"Which you got from—?"

"Th' kid! An' she didn't know what she was doin', either.

Listen! Svan might have *given* her the Buddha! I mean, she's the finest merchandise I ever—"

"Spare me."

"Yeah, well— That idiot Columbo is snoopin' around again. Didn't seem to learn his lesson."

"*You* could learn a lesson, Jacky. You made yourself a bad enemy."

"Wha'd ya want me to do, go up for—?"

"I want you to be damned careful, is what I want you to do. Get out of the little-girl business, for a while anyway. That's small change, in the first place, and stupid dangerous in the second."

"What'm I supposed to live off of?"

"Well, you were living off your share of Svan's kickbacks. Right now— Put your hand under the table. That's ten thousand. Live off that for a while. And keep— Keep . . . Hell, can I say clean?"

FIFTEEN

THURSDAY, AUGUST 13—2:32 A.M.

Muriel Paul stretched and yawned at the foot of the steel stairs that came down from the second-floor balcony of the EconoLodge Motel. She glanced around the parking lot. The lights blinked on a '94 Mazda MX-6, and she walked toward that car.

"Hey, kid," said the man behind the wheel. "Have a tough night?"

"Well— A hundred bucks is a hundred bucks. A girl does get tired, though."

"Get in. We got somethin' to celebrate."

Muriel got in. "What we got to celebrate, Jake?" she asked. "Somethin' good? Where'd you get the car?"

"Just guess where I got the car. We'll dump it later. I got somethin' to show ya."

He reached into the backseat and lifted a shopping bag into the front. She stared down into the bag and saw it was half filled with money. But on top of the money, some of it sinking down into the bills, were other things: what looked like—what *was*—jewelry. Her eyes widened as she saw necklaces and bracelets and rings. He thrust his left hand in front of her, and she saw a Concord gold watch with a circle of diamonds set around the dial.

"You can count the money while I drive."

"Jake—?"

"Yeah, I know. You've asked the question before. No, nobody was home. Tricky alarm, but I beat it. Hell, those people had *everything!* Wall-size TV, stereo equipment, what looked to me like pretty damned expensive paintings hanging all over. If I'd had time, or if I'd had some way to haul it, I could have taken silverware and a gun collection and god knows what all else. But I picked this stuff up in three bedrooms and was out of the house in less than five minutes."

Muriel began to count the money. "These are all hundreds," she whispered. "God, there's got to be *thousands and thousands* here!"

"Can ya figure? In a dresser drawer. Must be somethin' to be so rich you can be that careless."

"Figure it another way. People who keep this much cash around are probably cheating on their taxes."

"Well . . . right. Yeah, prob'ly. There was prob'ly more stashed somewhere. Maybe I should have taken time to look around more."

"No. You were right to grab and run. The longer you stay, the riskier."

She had counted more than six thousand dollars when they abruptly realized they were in big trouble. Three black-and-whites with flashing red and blue lights had appeared out of nowhere. For a brief moment Muriel wondered if the police were on their way somewhere else and had pulled up around the Mazda by chance. But it wasn't so.

Jake stopped. He had no choice. A minute later he and

Muriel were handcuffed, hands behind their backs, and a cop was reading them their rights.

"Uh, let me have a couple of hard-boiled eggs and a cup of coffee," said Columbo.

"Toast?" the waitress asked.

"No. No, thanks."

"The man is strange," Captain Sczciegel explained. "He's got a rep for it."

"I'm strange, too," said Hal Berwyn. "I'd like a gin Bloody Mary to start with. Then scrambled eggs, sausage, toast, and coffee."

Berwyn had asked Columbo and the captain to meet for breakfast. It was time, he suggested, to come to some conclusions about the Gunnar Svan murder. They weren't under pressure exactly, but time was running.

"Explain to me," he said when the waitress had left the table, "why you don't think Karlsen is the likeliest suspect."

"Well, uh— Okay. To start with, what was his motive?" Columbo asked.

"The man had abused his daughter," said Berwyn. "Motive for most men."

"Yeah, well, Ingrid went to Arizona on the second of July. Karlsen went down there and made his daughter come home on the twelfth. Karlsen went to see Mrs. Cooper-Svan on the twenty-first. Svan was murdered on the thirtieth. If he was mad—as mad as I'd have been if somebody had done what Svan did to *my* daughter when she was seventeen—he wouldn't have waited all that time."

Berwyn shook his head. "Two objections. In the first place, sometimes things stick in people's minds, and they get angrier and angrier. In the second place, maybe he was waiting to see if Svan was really going to put Ingrid in a movie. You know, he said on the tape he could forgive if she got what she wanted out of Gunnar."

Sczciegel shook his head. "I don't like your second objection. Nobody could be dumb enough to think a film director was going to put a girl in a film just because he'd banged her. Karlsen doesn't impress me as that dumb."

Berwyn shrugged. "If you think so. What about the phony alibi that Karlsen made up? That some woman called him and asked him to meet her that night. That's plain phony. Huh? Plain phony."

"Exactly right," said Columbo. "I've talked with Piers Karlsen. He's not stupid. Remember, if he killed Svan he didn't do it in a fit of anger. He had to plan it. Now, I ask ya, would a smart man rely on a dumb alibi like that? An anonymous woman he can't identify calls him and makes a proposition? Gimme a break!"

"Then why'd he say it?" Berwyn asked.

"Because an anonymous woman *did* call him and make a proposition."

"Columbo—?"

"To set him up."

The waitress brought Berwyn's Bloody Mary and poured coffee for Sczciegel and Columbo. "Sir," she said to Columbo. "The chef says he hasn't got any hard-boiled eggs. He can boil some, but it'll take twenty minutes or so."

"That's okay. I've got a couple of my own, here in my pocket. I'll just have the coffee."

Berwyn's eyes widened as he watched Columbo pull the two eggs from his raincoat and put them on the table. "I'll be damned."

"He has a glass of orange juice in the other pocket," said Sczciegel.

"And finding the Buddha in his car doesn't convince you?" Berwyn asked. "My god, Columbo! He had the Buddha in his automobile!"

"I might have been nearer to bein' convinced if we hadn't got another anonymous phone call. That was awful convenient, wasn't it?"

"Alright. What about Mrs. Cooper-Svan's tape?"

"So he was mad, and he blustered."

"Columbo's got a couple of other ideas," said the captain dryly.

"Yeah, and one of them I don't like a bit. I'm tryin' very hard to make it somebody else."

"Somebody gave up a million-dollar jade statuette," said Berwyn.

Columbo nodded. "Maybe. But what would *you* give up to avoid a murder conviction and a life sentence?"

3

9:21 A.M.

The three men had finished their breakfasts when Martha Zimmer came into the restaurant.

"Gentlemen," she said breathlessly. "They said I'd find

you here. This will interest all of you. Guess who's in jail this morning? For burglary. Muriel Paul!"

When Columbo arrived at the interrogation room, Muriel was sobbing. Wearing blue coveralls over a white T-shirt, she was chained to the table with a cuff on her left wrist. A half-eaten egg sandwich lay on a paper plate in front of her, and she had drunk half a cup of coffee. Two detectives, a man and a woman from Burglary, waited with apparent patience for her to stop crying. But she didn't stop.

"Hiya. Lieutenant Columbo. Homicide."

The woman nodded. "Bennett. Burglary. This is Zaferakes."

"Uh—?" Columbo pointed at Muriel.

"She's been a good girl," said Bennett. "She's given us a statement."

"What happen?"

"Her boyfriend, a small-timer named Jake Nixon, went big-time last night and broke into a home in Brentwood. He thought he'd defeated the alarm, but in fact what he did was set off a silent alarm. The first unit that responded followed his Mazda on a hunch. The second unit confirmed the burglary. The watch commander decided to lay back and not make him right off. Maybe he'd lead us to his fence. What he led us to was a motel where Muriel was working. By then we had the number off the Mazda and knew it was a stolen car. So we moved in on him. Muriel was busy doing an inventory of the take. She had cash in her lap and—"

Columbo shook his head. "Muriel— A boyfriend who's a burglar."

Muriel looked up. She wiped her eyes with her fists.

"You want to add to your statement somethin' about the house on Loma Vista Drive?"

"What's this about, Lieutenant?" asked Zaferakes. "Loma Vista—?"

"The house on Loma Vista Drive, where Muriel used to visit in her professional capacity, was heisted for a million dollars, and a man was killed. Muriel was in the house and prob'ly cased the place pretty thoroughly."

"I had nothin' to do with that!"

"Did you have a key to the house on Loma Vista?"

"No!"

"But you saw the jade Buddha. You knew it was there. You knew it was worth a million."

"And I read in the paper that it's back with Mrs. Cooper-Svan. Whoever heisted it didn't come out too well, did he? She's got it! The rich get richer, and the poor get poorer. And I get busted. Whoever took it didn't get a thing out of it."

"Maybe. Maybe not. Maybe somebody paid the guy that heisted it a nice piece of money."

"And that guy killed Gunnar? It would take a nice piece of money to do that."

"Your boyfriend is a smart burglar."

"Smart?" She shook the chain on her left wrist. "If he's so smart, why am I here?"

"Why are you, ya figure?"

"The dummy set off an alarm. Then he leads the cops to me. I didn't have anything to do with it until I got in the car and he shows me—"

"That's her statement, Lieutenant," said Bennett. "She knew nothing about the burglary until she got in his car and he showed her the loot. She was counting the money for him when our units stopped them. She'll testify that way. We won't need her testimony, really. You ought to see the watch Jake was wearing when we made him!"

At his desk Columbo found a note saying Miss Cabot in Juvenile was anxious to see him. He went over there.

"We have a man in custody," she said.

"A man—?"

"The man who beat up on Trish Miller."

Columbo frowned. "Hey! That's quick."

"Easy enough. We went out to the motel and put muscle on people who were paid to keep their mouths shut. They caved in quick and gave us the name of the guy who rented the room that night."

"I'd think he'd use a fake name."

"He did. But they recognized him. He'd been there before. Would you believe Vic Huggins?"

"The football player?"

"The same. And scared out of his wits. It's the end of him. Sex with a sixteen-year-old girl and—"

"He didn't have sex with her, actually. Did he?"

"No, not really. But he'd bought her for that. And he beat up on her."

"Maybe he didn't know how old she was. She looks old enough."

"What are you sayin', Lieutenant? You *sympathize* with this guy?"

"No way."

"You're gonna like this. He's given a statement naming Jacky Di Giacomo as the pimp. He says he gave Jacky five thousand dollars to quiet everything down. Jacky took the

girl and scrammed, the way she told us. A unit is out picking him up right now."

"I wanted to get him on somethin' else."

"I know you did. But we can't just overlook this and let
him go on doing what he's doing, not even for one more day.
We've got him cold on this one. Cold. The girls might not
make good witnesses against him; some smart lawyer
could tie them in knots. But Vic Huggins—? And he's going
to cooperate one hundred percent."

12:22 P.M.

"Time was, I didn't shoot this game so bad," said Captain
Sczciegel. "I've been warned against the chili, though. The
guy says he makes a hamburger."

Columbo nodded. He had come to Burt's to take refuge
and think, but someone had told the captain where to find
him.

"It's all coming unstuck," said Sczciegel. "I don't like the
way it's turning, do you?"

"No. No, I sure don't."

"Break, Columbo. Lemme see if I can still play. I used
to—"

Columbo broke the balls but didn't make anything. The
captain stepped up and sank the one, two, and three.

"I b'lieve you've played this game before," said Columbo.
He missed the four.

"Your heart isn't in it. I don't want you being too conspicuous in the interrogation of Di Giacomo. I guess you
know why."

"What'll he get for corruptin' a minor?"

"Ten years."

"Not much, considerin'."

"It'll finish him, Columbo. He's fifty years old. He'll be in as a sex offender who used little girls. He'll do hard time."

"I may still be able to make him in the Gunnar Svan case. I don't like the alternative."

"Don't stick your neck out, my friend. Do what you have to do."

1:10 P.M.

Ai-ling liked to have lunch at the Pacifica Club, because she could eat outdoors and could smoke, as she couldn't in most restaurants in Los Angeles. She sat at a poolside table in her iridescent-blue bikini, smoked a Marlboro, and sipped from a margarita.

Link came. "I've got news, if you haven't heard it," he said. "The police arrested Jacky Di Giacomo this morning. Morals charge."

"Well— Good thing Gunnar's dead. He did a lot of business with the formidable Mr. Di Giacomo. That's how he got Ingrid Karlsen."

"Are you sure of that?"

"That slimy bastard used to come to the house—when I wasn't there. But one day my father came by. He knew who Di Giacomo was, and he told me he'd seen 'Jacky' at my house. You know what he was doing? He was showing off a little girl to Gunnar! I wouldn't be surprised if Gunnar bought her, too."

"The man deserves to be dead."

"You just now figuring that out?"

Link nodded toward the gate. "Miss Boswell— Right?"

Ai-ling introduced Adrienne to Link, identifying him as "my shrink."

Adrienne sat down. "Big day in LA," she said. "Di Giacomo's in custody. Muriel Paul's in custody. Neither of them for anything to do with the murder, but—"

"The best place to have suspects," said Link. "Locked up in jail."

"I'm afraid it's not our friend Columbo who got them there," said Adrienne. "Di Giacomo's in for corrupting the morals of a minor—"

"Ingrid Karlsen?" Ai-ling asked.

"As a matter of fact, no. And Muriel Paul's in as accessory to a burglary in Brentwood."

"And Karlsen's out on bail," Ai-ling sneered.

"Well . . . You can bet Columbo's got something in mind. I've watched him work long enough to know that anybody who's committed murder is in peril with him on the case."

Ai-ling glanced hard at Link. "Well," she said. "Enough of that. I asked you to lunch because I want you to see the layout of your article."

7

2:32 P.M.

Columbo spoke with Muriel through the bars of a holding cell.

"They bring ya lunch?" he asked.

"Oh, yeah. If I gotta go to jail, get me out to Sybil Brand. Get me outa here."

"Ya know your jails, Muriel."

She sat on her bunk, looking up at him. "I've been in 'em before."

"I buy your story that you didn't know anything about the Brentwood burglary till Jake shows up with the loot. I think Burglary buys it, too. It's happened to you before. You're too trusting, Muriel. But— There's one thing that gets you in deep if you know anything about it and don't tell us."

"Which is the murder of Gunnar Svan," she said. She got up and leaned against the bars. "Which I had nothing to do with. Which Jake had nothing to do with. The night that happened I was working at JUST DONUTS."

"Yeah, but—"

"And Jake didn't have anything to do with it, either. You wanta know why? 'Cause Jake was in the county jail! The idiot had mugged a drunk and was doin' six months. He didn't get out till last week. So right off he steals a car and burglarizes a house! And gets me caught with the loot. That's the facts, Columbo. The record is there. Jake didn't heist the jade Buddha. And he didn't kill Gunnar Svan. And neither did I, and I didn't have anything to do with it."

8

3:02 P.M.

"Well, if it isn't my ol' pal, Lieutenant Columbo," said Jacky Di Giacomo. "Hey! You got a murder to stick on me, Columbo?"

Di Giacomo wore jail blue, handcuffs with a belly chain, and leg irons. He sneered at Columbo.

"I'm lookin' for one," said Columbo grimly.

"I bet you are. Nothin' you'd like better. I'll have the same lawyers, Columbo."

"For what? Some murder charge I might have against you, or just the charges they got about your doin' nasty things to little girls?"

"That's all a mistake," said Di Giacomo. "Those girls will explain. Uncle Jacky never did anything bad to them. Uncle Jacky was just a friend."

Columbo shrugged. "Not my problem. But I guess the evidence is there that you sent Ingrid Karlsen over to Arizona. There's evidence, too, that you were inside the Cooper-Svan residence and saw the jade Buddha."

Di Giacomo sneered again. "If I'd heisted the Buddha, I'd have it, wouldn't I? Or'd have fenced it. But I hear it's back in the possession of Mrs. Cooper-Svan."

Columbo sighed and nodded. "Y' ever been in San Quentin, Jacky?"

Di Giacomo blanched. "No. Hell, no."

"I hear they don't like guys that come in there for messin' with little girls. You might be better off there on a murder charge."

"Oh, sure, Columbo. Nice try. I'll plead guilty to killing Gunnar Svan. Forget it."

9

4:02 P.M.

Pamela Murphy sat in an interrogation room as Muriel had earlier, with one wrist chained to the table. She was not tearful as Muriel had been. She was angry and defiant, with her chained fist clenched.

Columbo asked the other detectives to leave the room and let him talk to her alone.

"Y' know why you're here?" he asked her.

"Who the hell knows? *They* don't know. *I* don't know. *You* know?"

"Yeah, I know. Right now, you're here because you sent a seventeen-year-old girl to Arizona to engage in sex with Gunnar Svan—for which Jacky Di Giacomo was paid, and you got part of the money. And to make it more interesting, you went over to Arizona and took part in a threesome—for which you were paid more. That's what's called corruptin' a minor. Sometimes it's called child abuse."

"I wasn't paid anything."

"Maybe. You can explain to the jury why Gunnar Svan gave you a BMW."

"For *me!*" she said, her eyes glittering. "For what *I* did! Not for any children."

"There'll be evidence the other way. None of which is my particular business. My business is homicide. What I need to know is, who killed Gunnar Svan? If you can help me out with that, I can help you out."

"What you want me to say is that Jacky did it."

"If he did. Only if he did."

"Well, Lieutenant Columbo, on the night when Gunnar was murdered, Jacky was in the club, ogling the dancers— me and the others. There were half a dozen witnesses, at least half a dozen, who'll testify to that. Jacky won't need some little schoolteacher on that one. There's *plenty* of evidence. *Plenty.* You're gonna have to look someplace else, Columbo."

"Which leaves me with just one suspect, Cap'n."

"Besides Karlsen."

"Besides Karlsen."

Captain Sczciegel shook his head. "Make sure you've got it cold, Columbo. We can't afford a screwup on this one."

"Right. I figure we have to set up a confrontation. We'll need Berwyn there. Meantime, I'll do some final checkin'. I don't like it, Cap'n. You know I don't like it. But there it is. What else is there?"

Sczciegel nodded. "I see you're carrying your sidearm."

"Yes, sir."

"Is it loaded?"

"Well, I got the bullets in the car, Cap'n. I figure I can put 'em in when I need 'em."

SIXTEEN

Fog lay heavily over the beach. Even Dog's enthu-
siasm was damped by the thick clouds of it that drifted in
off the sea. The gulls did not strut but prowled the beach
sullenly. When Dog charged after one, it did not wait until
the last moment before lifting into the air but flew when
it first noticed him coming, as if it was in no mood for his
game.

Columbo sat on a bench. He puffed on a cigar and stared
at the waves rolling slowly in, propelled by no great wind.
Foghorns bellowed out at sea. Besides himself, the only
other person on the beach was a surf-caster who was ex-
periencing some success and dropped little fish in his
bucket. When he caught a big fish, he looked at it dis-
dainfully, apparently decided it was inedible, pulled out
the hook, and tossed it into the surf.

Columbo had not slept. All night he had lain half awake,
sometimes entirely awake, his mind possessed by a star

drill with no dust, a shard of glass beyond the stoop, an audiotape that began and ended at just the right time, anonymous telephone calls at suspiciously convenient moments—

He disliked the way it all fit together. He disliked it more than a little. But whichever way he turned it, it came out the same.

The surf-caster picked up his bucket and walked toward Columbo.

"You're Columbo, the homicide guy, aren't you?"

Columbo looked up into a bland, honest, black face. He nodded. "Guilty."

"Saw you on television. You got a great job. Me, I'm an auto mechanic, got a little service station." He nodded toward the Peugeot. "That yours?"

"That's mine."

"One of the best cars ever built. Love to work on that car. 'Course, ya gotta jury-rig 'em now, use whatever parts ya can get. You need work done on that car—" The fisherman reached in his pocket and handed Columbo a card printed with the name Alonzo Willard. "You bring her in. I'm one of the few guys in town that knows anything about those cars."

Columbo grinned. "What I'd rather, you'd fry me a mess of fish—fresh, like you got there. I love what comes from the ocean."

"You'd like a mess of fresh fish? You give me a call, come to my house. Missus, she'd love to fry a mess of fish for you. Got a wife? Bring your wife."

"You like lasagna?" Columbo asked. "Mrs. C makes great lasagna. Dinner at your house, fish. Dinner at my house, lasagna. I'll call ya. I really will."

The surf-caster nodded with an enthusiastic smile.

"Lookin' forward to it. When I tell my wife we're gonna have dinner with a homicide detective!"

8:02 A.M.

Muriel was resigned and docile. She extended her left hand toward the guard and submitted quietly to being cuffed to the long chain. She was third from last in line, and shortly the line of ten moved on: women on their way to a bus that would haul them to court.

She had made up her mind. She would plead guilty. She was supposed to talk to a public defender first, but she saw no reason to string things out. She was a sucker and had got caught again. Maybe prison was where she belonged, where she couldn't get in trouble. It didn't make any difference what she decided or where she belonged; she was on her way. She knew it, and she knew there was nothing she could do about it.

Pam was on the same bus, hooked to another chain. She was in a very different mood. She had talked to a lawyer. She had money to pay him, and she was going to fight. She had to. If they made their charges stick, she'd be too old for her profession by the time she got out.

Damn Di Giacomo! Damn that stupid son of a bitch! It would have been better if they'd killed Svan and heisted the Buddha. They could have gotten away with that. This— A *morals* charge! Too damned many witnesses! For a stupid damned pimping operation!

3

Guards walked up and down a cell block at County Jail. They were missing a man. The count wasn't right.

"Cap'n— We found him. Di Giacomo. He's not dead, but he's not far from it. Beat— God!"

The captain shook his head. He glanced at the prisoners standing in a line in front of their cells. "They don't like guys that do bad things to little girls," he said.

4

10 : 1 1 A.M.

In her office, Ai-ling spoke to her attorney on the telephone—

"I've been asked to meet with Columbo and Sczciegel and Berwyn at four this afternoon. You should be there, hmm?"

The lawyer's name was Martin Landsittle. "Why do they want to talk to you?"

"To clear up a few points, Columbo said."

"He suggest what points?"

"He said just a few little things that were bothering him."

"Well, I tell you, Ai-ling, if you bring a lawyer to this conference, you do create an adversary situation. It suggests you think you are a suspect. Are you?"

"God only knows. Columbo is— Well, I suppose you've heard of him."

"More than heard of him."

"Well, what do I do?"

"See him without me. But remember this. There's an old police cliché that goes, 'Talkers never walk, and walkers never talk.' Answer questions you want to answer. Don't volunteer anything. And if they seem to be backing you into a corner, tell them you want to see your lawyer. That stops the interrogation, automatically and for sure."

"Okay. And— Hey, Martin . . . Am I smarter than any cop on the Los Angeles Police Department, or aren't I?"

Landsittle was silent on the line for a moment. Then he said—"Ai-ling, do you need to be?"

5

12:32 P.M.

Adrienne looked up from a plate of veal and pasta—the same that she had recommended to Columbo and he had ordered, too—and shook her head.

"I've never seen a man looking more miserable," she said.

Columbo nodded. "And I can't tell ya why. Even journalistic ethics won't cover."

"You know what happened to Di Giacomo this morning," she said. "They're not sure he'll live. Strange, isn't it? Crooks in jails and prisons have a strict sense of honor and morality. You don't squeal. You don't abuse little girls. You come in with one of those on your record—"

"Yeah . . . I didn't *want* the guy that way, Adrienne. I

wanted him to be true and fair convicted."

"I understand. You've got an old-fashioned sense of right and wrong, Columbo. With you, the end doesn't justify the means."

Columbo sipped from a glass of dark-red wine. "I guess that's philosophy. 'End doesn't justify . . .' Yeah. Right. In my line of work, you gotta do some things you can't like very much; but when ya do 'em, you gotta be sure you do 'em right. You can't live with it if you take shortcuts."

"You don't take shortcuts, Columbo. I've watched you and seen that you don't."

He blew a loud sigh. "This is a miserable day, Adrienne."

4:02 P.M.

"This is an informal meeting, Mrs. Cooper-Svan," said Hal Berwyn, the assistant district attorney. "We would like to tie up some loose ends in the investigation into the death of your husband. Even though it's informal, you are entitled to have counsel present if you wish. Also, with your consent, we would like to record the meeting on videotape."

"That's a bit formidable," said Ai-ling. "Maybe I *should* have my attorney present."

"We can break right now and wait for him," said Berwyn.

She glanced around the conference room. Columbo was there, looking confused and seedy as always—but, she was sure, as quick and dangerous as a rattlesnake. Captain Sczciegel: not a very impressive sort of fellow. Berwyn. She didn't feel challenged by him.

Ai-ling shrugged. She was wearing a black dress with padded shoulders, a short skirt, and deep cleavage. "Since I have nothing to hide— Let's have our meeting, Mr. Berwyn."

"Okay. You know Lieutenant Columbo. Since he's the man who has conducted the investigation, we'll let him do most of the talking."

Columbo turned up the palms of his hands. "Talkin' is not one of my strong suits. So— Maybe everybody will be patient with me. I've been working two full weeks now on the investigation into the death of Mr. Gunnar Svan. There are some points that just sort of hang open and don't explain themselves. I don't know any other way to run an investigation than to close all those kinds of points."

"I imagine," said Ai-ling, "that one of those points is, why was a bit of glass from the back door lying out in the yard?"

"I've wondered about that," said Columbo.

"So have I, Lieutenant. I wonder if the answer isn't that the murderer, hurrying out of the house, accidentally kicked that one piece of glass out the door."

Columbo turned down the corners of his mouth and nodded. "That's a good idea," he said. "That would explain that, for sure."

"It explains it for me," said Ai-ling.

Columbo ran his hand through his hair. "Hey. Y' see? That's how we get things cleared up. That's the point here: to clean up little points. So . . . Mrs. Cooper-Svan, Mr. Svan was stealing money from you, in considerable amounts, isn't that true?"

Ai-ling stiffened and glared. "Does that mean you think I killed him, because he was stealing from me? Do I suddenly find myself a suspect?"

Columbo shook his head. "Whenever a person is murdered, the husband or wife is a suspect, automatically.

You've always been a suspect, Mrs. Cooper-Svan. But maybe you shouldn't be. You explained the glass thing right off. But, uh, he *was* stealin' from you, regularly. Right?"

"My accountant is beginning to straighten that out. I'd guessed he was stealing. I suspected. I had no idea how much."

"And some of the money went to . . . bad girls. And to a procurer."

"I suspected that, too. I didn't know it."

"Well— Mrs. Cooper-Svan, what was the murder weapon? Do you know?"

"Of course not."

"I do. It was a tool that was in your house. The murderer didn't bring it in; it was there. It's a tool called a star drill, a heavy steel bar with a pointy end. Somebody brought it up from the basement, killed Mr. Svan with it, and took it back down to the basement—but not before washing the blood off it."

"What makes you think so?" she asked.

"Well," said Columbo, "everything else in that room in the basement was covered with dust. The star drill was clean. Somebody'd washed it off. Now, what I can't figure out is, why would a guy that came to the house with the intention of killing Mr. Svan and stealing the Buddha not be carryin' his own weapon? Why would he go down in the basement and find a star drill—which is not somethin' you'd find in most houses—use it, and then clean it off?"

"There are a lot of assumptions behind that question, Lieutenant. How do we know the workman didn't wipe off the star drill for some reason?"

"We know because we asked him," said Columbo. "Sergeant Zimmer went to see your contractor and asked that question."

"I gather this leads you to some conclusion," said Ai-ling coldly.

"I have to follow the facts where they lead, Ma'am."

"The facts didn't seem to lead very far with Piers Karlsen. Apart from the fact that the Buddha was found in his car, he did come to my office and threaten my husband—which threat I taped."

"That's another loose end I'd like to tie up." Columbo opened a file folder and pulled out a few sheets of paper fastened together with a paper clip. "This is a typed-up transcript of what Karlsen said on that tape. Looka what he says. I mean, look at the underlined part."

> "I'm saying your husband is corrupting my daughter."
>
> " 'Corrupting'? Please?"
>
> "Mrs. Svan— I told you. To put the matter in the bluntest words, your forty-year-old husband is fucking my seventeen-year-old daughter!"

"'Y' see what I got in mind?" Columbo asked. "He says, 'I'm saying.' He says, 'I told you.' What we've got on this tape is less than everything that was said. You didn't edit this tape in some way, did you, Mrs. Cooper-Svan?"

"*Lieutenant*— When he began to bluster and threaten, I turned on the recorder. When he'd made his threat, I turned it off. I suppose I see what you're driving at. But that's the explanation."

Columbo nodded. "Okay. I'm glad to get that point cleared up."

"Are there any further points?" she asked.

"Well— Just a couple. May not amount to anything at all."

"I'm hoping to be home in time for dinner," said Ai-ling.

"Dinner. That does bring up another small point. The evening when Mr. Svan was killed, you had dinner with Adrienne Boswell. Right?"

"I did, yes."

"At Umberto's. Now, I'm interested of course in the times when things happened that night. Adrienne says you came into Umberto's a few minutes after eight and apologized for being late. So, what does that make it: five minutes after eight, ten minutes after eight?"

"It was more than five minutes. If I'd only been five minutes late, I wouldn't have apologized. But it wasn't fifteen minutes, either, because I'd have stopped and phoned if I'd been *that* late."

"Okay, say ten after. Okay? Now, how long would it take to drive from your house to Umberto's?"

"About half an hour."

"Right. That's what it took me when I tried it. So you left home by, say, seven-thirty, seven-forty?"

Ai-ling nodded. "I suppose so."

"Okay. Uh . . . Oh, say. A curious thing, Mrs. Cooper-Svan. Adrienne says you ate a full dinner at Umberto's— antipasto, veal scaloppine, dessert, coffee. Right?"

Ai-ling smiled faintly and nodded. "And Sambuca with a coffee bean in the glass. Always at Umberto's."

"But you had just eaten a full meal at home."

"What makes you think I did?"

"The meal Mrs. Yasukawa had prepared was all eaten up. There were two sets of dirty dishes in the dishwasher."

"I sat down at the table with Gunnar. I nibbled a bit. *He* ate most of the lasagna and the salad. Drinking made him hungry. He really gorged himself."

"I'm afraid not, Mrs. Cooper-Svan. When he did the autopsy, Dr. Culp found a normal meal in Mr. Svan's stomach—normal, that is, except for an excessive quantity of alcohol."

"Well— I scraped my plate into the disposal."

"Which is it, Mrs. Cooper-Svan?" asked Captain Sczciegel. "Your husband gorged himself or you put a lot of food through the disposal?"

"It's difficult to remember. That was a difficult night."

Ai-ling sat now with her chair pushed back a little, leaning forward on her elbows. Though no one could see it, she had spread her legs and let her skirt ride up. The posture did, though, afford the three men a distracting view of her cleavage.

Columbo ran his hands over his face. "I'd guess that was a tough night. I'd guess things would be tough to remember."

"She remembers the coffee bean in the Sambuca," said Sczciegel.

"Maybe I didn't get a coffee bean in the Sambuca," said Ai-ling sullenly. "Maybe I didn't even have Sambuca. You always do at Umberto's. On the house. Maybe that's why—"

"I'm more interested in somethin' else, Mrs. Cooper-Svan. I'm tryin' to get the time sequence straight in my mind. Now, you left your office between five-thirty and five-forty-five. Your secretary confirms that. The garage boy who brought your car up confirms it. What's it take you to get home? Twenty minutes? Half an hour?"

"Between the one and the other."

"Which means you didn't get home much before six, did you?"

"I got home about six, I suppose."

"And left about an hour and a half later. Or an hour and forty minutes."

"Yes."

"Mrs. Cooper-Svan, you and I and Adrienne Boswell had lunch at the Pacifica Club a week ago today. Adrienne asked you a question I would never have asked. She asked how it had been between you and Mr. Svan. I mean, she asked if you—" He made a circle in the air with his right hand. "You know what I mean."

"The question was whether Gunnar and I were still intimate—meaning, I suppose, did I forgive him for the dumb things he was doing. Were we still a loving couple?"

"And what was your answer?"

"I told you that very night, the night he was killed, he and I had a complete intimate experience."

"You said, as I remember, that he had exhausted you."

Ai-ling nodded and again managed to smile. "That's what I said."

Columbo shook his head. "I . . . I don't know how to ask questions like this." He glanced at Sczciegel, then at Berwyn. "But, okay, you couldn't be exhausted by just one— Uh . . . By just one . . . experience?"

"No, Lieutenant," she said with mock patience. "Gunnar— Well, how can I say it? He exhausted the both of us."

"Well, we got confirmation of it. The autopsy showed that Mr. Svan was for sure exhausted—I mean, in that way. I mean, he'd really— According to the medical examiner."

"That's what I told you, Lieutenant Columbo. Gunnar and I were still very much a loving couple. I knew he did some rotten things, but he made up for an awful lot." She wiped an eye with one finger. "He was in some ways a marvelous man."

Columbo shook his head. "There's somethin' wrong here. Mr. Gunnar Svan was sexually depleted when he died— But it wasn't because of anything he did with you. He'd had the kind of experience you're talkin' about, but not with you. He'd had it with Ingrid Karlsen, in his car, on a road out in the hills."

"*That's ridiculous!*" Ai-ling snapped. "Sure, he'd had times with that juvenile chippy, but on the night he died, he had times with *me!* What are you doing, taking her word for it?"

"No, Ma'am. The police lab guys found stuff on the front seat of Mr. Svan's car that prove they'd had sex together in the car."

"Maybe *sometime!*"

"She'll make a good witness, Ma'am—when her testimony is corroborated by the lab findings. But that's not the whole of it. Y' see, the *time* doesn't work. Mr. Svan had arrived not long before you did. In the regular course of an investigation, officers talk to all the neighbors. Two of them saw Mr. Svan's car come in about the same time yours did. So you were both home about six o'clock, or a few minutes after."

"And—?"

"When Mr. Svan died, he had a blood-alcohol level of point-one-nine. At six o'clock he arrived sober enough to drive his car. It takes *time* to get that drunk, Mrs. Cooper-Svan. If he'd gulped it all down in a few minutes, he'd have thrown it up. What's more, he had a variety of drinks in him: gin and wine and brandy. So we gotta figure, between six o'clock and seven-thirty, he ate a full meal, with wine and coffee and brandy. Besides that, he had in him a substantial amount of gin. He drank all that, ate all that, and still had time to make love with you, to the point of exhaustion? He must have been a busy man in that ninety minutes."

"As always, the explanation is perfectly simple, Lieutenant Columbo. A good part of what he drank, he drank after I left."

"Except for a coupla little things, Mrs. Cooper-Svan. In the first place, when he was found there was no glass or bottle in the room. In fact, the glasses were in the dishwasher, and the liquor was in its cabinet."

"Gunnar had a fetish for being neat," Ai-ling said weakly.

"Maybe so. But two times you described the way he was when you left the house. Once you used the word 'torpid.' Another time you used the words 'passed-out drunk.' You're asking us to believe that between six o'clock and seven-thirty he made love to you to the point of exhaustion, ate a complete meal, and drank himself into a stupor. I'm sorry, Mrs. Cooper-Svan. I wish I could believe it."

"I think I had better talk to my lawyer," she said.

Captain Sczciegel stepped to the door of the room. "Officer Tiegs," he said to a uniformed woman who was waiting outside, "we are placing Mrs. Cooper-Svan under arrest. Please make the arrest and read her her rights."

Officer Tiegs came in. She gestured to Ai-ling that she should stand. Stunned and drawing deep breaths, Ai-ling watched as the woman looped a chain around her waist and handcuffed her.

"You have a right to remain silent. Anything you say may be taken down in evidence and may be used against you—"

EPILOGUE

Ai-ling Cooper-Svan was confined in the women's jail, Sybil Brand Institute, on a charge of aggravated murder. The court refused to release her on bond. Her lawyer, Martin Landsittle, was an expert at plea-bargaining, also at generating publicity to win sympathy for his clients. For weeks the newspapers were filled with stories of Gunnar Svan's abuse of her trust and even of her person. Svan's association with people like Jacky Di Giacomo added to the impression that Ai-ling Cooper-Svan had acted under extreme provocation.

On November 18 she appeared in court, entered a plea of guilty to a reduced charge, and was sentenced to serve ten years in the California women's prison at Fontera. Her conduct as a prisoner has been exemplary, and she will almost certainly be released sometime in her seventh year.

She works in the kitchen and behind the food-serving line. Her job is to push carts of trays, dishes, and utensils to the serving line and unload them onto the counters, where the inmates can pick them up. The inmates scrape their plates into plastic bags mounted on carts and deposit their trays and dirty dishes and utensils in bins on other carts. Ai-ling pushes these carts into the dishwashing area. She does not wash dishes. Between meals she cleans the stainless-steel serving counter with a germicidal detergent. Others clean the tables and mop the floors.

The name of this kitchen orderly appears at the top of the *Glitz* masthead, thus—Ai-ling Cooper-Svan, publisher and editor-in-chief, 1988–1996. She still owns *Glitz,* and no one doubts she will return to full control as soon as she is released. Some think she never relinquished control.

A general rule of the prison is that an inmate cannot run a business. Ai-ling is allowed, even so, to keep up a voluminous correspondence with Bill Lloyd, who runs *Glitz* for her in her absence. He is on her list of authorized visitors and goes to see her monthly. She reads constantly and sends Lloyd suggestions about what celebrities the magazine should feature, what writers and photographers should be assigned to each job, how stories should be placed, and what advertising should be sought. He sends her photo proofs and drafts of articles. He brings the layouts of each issue. She reviews all these materials in her cell and writes long letters of instructions. She has changed *Glitz* significantly. Its coverage now pays more attention to political figures than it did before. A complimentary article in *Glitz* can contribute much to positioning a would-be candidate for a run for higher office. When the magazine published its first political endorsement, of a candidate for the Republican nomination for United States Senator, an editorial cartoon in a San Francisco

newspaper portrayed Ai-ling reaching out between cell
bars to dub the kneeling candidate a knight.

Because the case was so efficiently disposed of, Link
Hilliard was never questioned, never seriously suspected.
While Ai-ling was still in jail at Sybil Brand, he went to
the house and retrieved the Glock. Wearing gloves, he dis-
assembled it, wiped it clean of any fingerprints that might
possibly remain on it, then put it in his office trash, one
part at a time over a period of weeks. It is in a landfill.

The death of Ed Phillips remained an open file.
Columbo had a vague suspicion that Ai-ling had shot
him, but he had no evidence, and it was not his case.
Other detectives gave it more-than-perfunctory investigation but soon abandoned it. The man had not been,
after all, much of an asset to society; and very likely he
had been killed by someone who had caught him trying
to steal their car.

Jacky Di Giacomo recovered from his jailhouse beating
and was sentenced to ten to twenty-five years.

Pamela Murphy was sentenced to three to seven. She
was paroled after thirty-seven months. Her parole officer
will not allow her to strip for a living. She works as a
housekeeper in a Holiday Inn.

Muriel Paul was allowed to plead to a reduced charge
after she gave testimony against Jake Nixon. All told, she
spent fourteen months in Sybil Brand. She went back to
JUST DONUTS and turns an occasional trick, as before.

Vic Huggins, the professional football player who beat
up on Trish Miller, was sentenced to a year in jail. He was

banned from football for life, but the ban was lifted for the second season after his release.

Trish Miller remained on probation until she was eighteen. Immediately after termination of her probation she was arrested for shoplifting. Two months later she was arrested, again for shoplifting. She served six months in Sybil Brand and on her release married the brother of her cellmate. They moved to Iowa, where no one knew of her record—or of his; he had one, too. She gave birth to three children in rapid succession. Her mother sent her Di Giacomo's two thousand dollars, and it became part of the down payment on a small hatchery.

Ingrid Karlsen earned her high school equivalency certificate and enrolled at UCLA as a student of film and drama. When she decided to drop out, her father kicked her ass—literally. She graduated and is employed as an assistant casting director.

The article about Adrienne appeared on schedule in the October issue of *Glitz*—while Ai-ling was in jail. It had the impact Ai-ling had promised. No longer just a reporter, Adrienne was a *celebrity*. She appeared on every television talk show. She became the subject of tabloid stories—one of which implied she had a romantic attachment to Lieutenant Columbo, LAPD Homicide. She was hired to co-anchor a morning television news-and-talk show.

Her new status was too much for Dan the architect. He dropped away. It was not too much for Scott. He was a TV sportscaster, and he and Adrienne quickly became a celebrity pair.

Adrienne called Columbo early in January and invited him and Mrs. Columbo to attend a dinner she and Scott were having at Umberto's, for some twenty friends. Mrs. Columbo would have liked to go, but Columbo had to remind her they had already committed themselves to a fish dinner with their new friends, Mr. and Mrs. Alonzo Willard. Alonzo would be out casting for fresh fish, and it wouldn't do to disappoint him.